To Protect and Serve

Pat Adeff

Copyright © 2016 Pat Adeff

All rights reserved.

ISBN-10: 1493668803
ISBN-13: 978-1493668809

DEDICATION

This book is dedicated to my girls, Cat and Cryss.

I'm so very proud of you!

xxxooo
Mom

This book is also dedicated to the men and women of America's police force. Thank you for protecting and serving our communities; for putting your lives on the line. Mike, Dom, Sherrie, Stan, Alex, Diane, Randy…your compassion, humanity and dedication set the standard for police officers everywhere.

****

This is a work of fiction. Any resemblance to individuals, either living or dead, is purely from the author's imagination, not from real life.

ACKNOWLEDGEMENTS

A very special "Thank You" goes to Detective Dominick Povero of the Redlands Police Department for side-checking my writing so I sound like I know police procedure. Any and all mistakes are mine, not his. Also, thank you Dom for introducing me to Michael Connelly's work!

A special acknowledgement goes to my dad, James Craw, for believing in me. And for buying me a laptop for my writing! Love you! Trish

Thank you to my brother, Chuck, for giving me that wonderful cabin in Angeles Oaks, where I completed the first draft of this story.

Thank you to my other brother, Bill, for keeping me fed at The Gourmet Pizza Shoppe in Redlands, CA. Hungry authors don't write well.

A huge thank you to Ali Rafter and Noelle Kiely for their artistic insight and excellent editing.

And finally thank you, Todd, for finding me and becoming my own Doug Saunders. Next lifetime I'll find you sooner so I can love you longer.

COVER PHOTOGRAPHY BY JAMIE FISHER OF

Cover Models Guy La Brusciano and Stella Gina Lofgren

PROLOGUE

Doug could no longer feel the fingers of his left hand. His arm from shoulder to wrist was stiff and rapidly becoming numb. He could feel the sticky warmth of fresh blood oozing across his neck from the bullet wound in his shoulder. His heart was leaping in his chest; pulse pounding; breathing rapid, deep and desperate. His shoulder burned as though it was on fire.

He looked up from where he was inexplicably pinned on the blood-soaked ground and watched the life leaving the young woman's pleading eyes as the killer tightened his grip around her neck.

There was nothing Doug could do to prevent her death. Through the buzz in his ears, he could hear sirens from the back-up he'd called for, but he knew they'd be too late. He tried to summon enough strength to reach his gun. He was paralyzed with a fear greater than any he'd ever previously encountered in the line of duty. He felt helpless, powerless and useless.

"Let her go!" he pleaded. "Let her go, and walk away. Don't kill her. Just walk away." Doug knew he sounded like he was begging. He was.

Just as the outstretched fingers of his right hand touched his gun he heard a snap that sounded like the dry branch of a tree breaking, and watched the woman's lifeless body slide to the ground.

Although her eyes were open, he knew she was no longer there. His own vision started to grow dark around the edges. He heard the killer's boots crunch on the gravel.

Doug rolled onto his back and viewed the killer lean down close to him. He focused on the killer's gun positioned in front of his face. As though from a distance, he saw the killer's finger tighten on the trigger. Doug knew it would be the last thing he ever witnessed.

Then suddenly all was dark.

****

Doug opened his eyes and found himself in bed. His left arm was pinned beneath a smooth, tanned feminine neck and shoulder, which had caused his arm to fall asleep.

His heartbeat was heavy and bounding in his chest and his breath came rapidly.

Slowly extricating his arm, he sat up, the navy blue sheet pooling around his lean hips. He ran fingers through his short dark hair as he took a couple of cleansing breaths.

"Doug? You awake?" The feminine form behind him now sat up and ran a manicured hand around to the front of his broad chest until he could feel the warmth of her firm, sculptured breasts pressing against his back.

He pushed down a wave of revulsion that surprised him and put one of his hands over hers to stop its downward direction. He felt her stiffen against his back and then she pulled away from him.

Doug puzzled himself with the way he was acting. He shook it off, attributing it to the false emotion stirred up by the dream. That awful impotent dream.

It was his biggest fear as a cop. That he'd be unable to save someone in time. That the bad guy would win. It wasn't fear for his own life. He was comfortable with knowing that his life was on the line.

He would never be comfortable with knowing that he'd failed in the line of duty, and an innocent civilian would be dead. Like most other cops, he dreaded the possibility.

He shoved out of the bed and padded into the bathroom. He set the shower temp to hot and stepped under the needle spray. When the shower door opened behind him he wasn't surprised. Nor was he tempted. He knew that Jessica wouldn't understand, and would probably pretend to be hurt. He also knew she'd move on and find someone else.

They weren't in love; they liked each other and were convenient. Over the years, Doug just hadn't found anyone who made him feel strongly enough to commit. Once or twice he'd been in lust, but not in love. Jessica was just the latest in line.

Doug's day didn't improve when he arrived at the station, either. As a rule, he got along with most of the other officers. However, there was just something about the new sergeant that set his teeth on edge. On the outside, the guy seemed fine. A little too precise for Doug's taste, but better that than sloppy. Maybe it was the way the guy spoke – just this side of prissy. Maybe it was the way he didn't have a single hair out of place. Or maybe it was just the fact that he was an asshole. Yep. That was it. And now that Doug was able to correctly file that fact, he felt better.

Right up until said sergeant spoke to him.

"Saunders!"

Doug stopped in the hallway and backed up two paces to the open office door.

"Sir?"

"Come in. Come in." Another point against him; the guy repeated himself.

"Yes, Sir." Doug stood in front of the pristine desk and waited for the sergeant to speak.

"Doug, are we having a communication problem?" The sergeant's hands were folded together in the center of his desk.

"Sir?" Doug tried to hide his impatience. God only knew what had gotten the sergeant's knickers in a twist this time.

"Communication. Between us. It's lacking." The sergeant also seemed unable to speak in full sentences.

"How's that, Sir?" Doug tried to keep his expression neutral.

"Forms?" A single raised eyebrow accompanied the latest syllable. The brow looking suspiciously plucked – or maybe waxed.

"Forms, Sir?" Doug was beyond understanding at this point.

"Forms. Requisition forms, to be precise."

God forbid we not be precise.

"Sir. I'm at a loss here. Please remind me." Doug hoped that the grimace around his mouth might pass for a small smile.

No such luck.

"Don't get smart with me, Saunders. I'm onto your game." Obviously the good sergeant knew something Doug didn't.

"Sir, I'm not trying to get smart with you. I honestly don't know what you're talking about." Doug tried for a little sincerity in his voice and demeanor.

It seemed to work, because the sergeant actually started explaining himself. Apparently Doug had failed to fill in one of the myriad requisite forms. As the sergeant continued to explain in exquisitely gruesome detail about the form, Doug's mind wandered.

He had a meeting today with Jorge Morales, a young man who was working undercover in one of the local gangs. Last year when Jorge tried to leave the gang, he'd been beaten and kicked right up to death's door. After a painful and terror-filled recovery, Jorge decided to get even. Although dangerous, his plan was good. He "remained" in the gang and was working on getting information regarding their drug sales in order to get the leaders put behind bars. Since there were a couple of deaths involved, there was a good chance he could get them put away for life.

Doug came back to the present and realized that he'd apparently been listening to silence, and for quite some time according to the look on the sergeant's face.

"Are we clear, Saunders?"

"Crystal, Sir. Will there be anything else?"

"No. It is what it is."

Doug winced inwardly. NO one liked that hackneyed phrase. And no one used it more often than the Sergeant.

"Dismissed."

With that, Doug headed out the door and down the hall to the locker room. What an ass. Could this day get any worse?

Of course it could.

Doug was supposed to meet Jorge at a downtown parking structure. After waiting 45 minutes, Doug had the awful gut feeling that something bad had happened. He headed back to the police department and asked one of the bilingual officers to call Jorge's number and check on him.

By the look on Crystal's face, Doug knew something VERY bad had happened. "Doug, I'm sorry. That was his aunt. Jorge's in the hospital. He was shot last night. They've got him in ICU."

Doug commandeered a black and white, again forgetting the requisition forms, and flew over to Chapman Hospital. When the elevator doors opened on the ICU floor, Doug was looking into the eyes of Armando, the main leader of the gang Jorge had 'joined.'

With recognition, but without speaking, they passed each other. Doug stepped out of the elevator and into the hallway while the gang leader stepped into the elevator. Eye contact was maintained while the elevator doors shut. Just before the doors met, Doug saw Armando's middle finger thrust into the air. Shaking his head, Doug thought to himself that once again, someone was telling him that he was number one. Too bad they keep forgetting to use the correct finger.

Doug turned and went down to the nurses' station and asked which curtain area Jorge was in. Emily, one of Doug's ex-girlfriends, smiled and pointed out the area at the end of the unit.

He quietly moved down to the area and glanced around the corner of the curtain to ensure that no other visitors were present. When he saw that it was all clear, he stepped next to Jorge's bed.

Jorge appeared to be asleep. His mouth was slightly open and his head was rolled away from Doug. Looking closer, Doug felt the hairs on the back of his neck stand up. The monitor had been turned off. Jorge wasn't breathing. And the handle of a four inch blade knife was sticking out of his side, surrounded by a spreading pool of red.

Doug yelled for the nurse and within seconds the curtain was thrust aside, as was Doug, and three people started working on Jorge. CPR – Intubation – Three units type-specific blood. Atropine, Lidocaine, Epinephrine, calcium bicarbonate and more epinephrine all injected into the IV line.

"200 joules!" ... 250... 300... 350... The doctor tried valiantly to get a pulse, but to no avail.

Doug winced when he saw the doctor open Jorge's chest for a thoracotomy. There was blood everywhere. The crunching of the ribs under the surgeon's tool made Doug swallow several times trying to keep breakfast down. After what seemed like an eternity of gory chaos, the attending doctor called time of death at 9:44 am.

Yep, the day had definitely gotten worse.

PAT ADEFF

CHAPTER 1

"Why the hell not."

It wasn't exactly what Nancy wanted to say at that moment, but other words failed her. She knew that later some witty remark would come to mind, but by then it would be too late. Typical.

She looked around the family-style restaurant and noticed that everything seemed slightly unreal. It wasn't weird like Dali's melting clocks. It was real life ... just sharpened a notch like they do in some movies to give it an edge.

The man and woman sitting at the table to the left were in their 70's and having a pleasant conversation about a cruise they were planning. It was sweet – they were even holding hands. The mother and father across the aisle in the large booth were laughing at something their young son had said. Nancy watched as the father reached out and affectionately ruffled the child's hair.

A waitress walked by with her arms laded with hot food and set plates in front of some teenagers in the booth directly across from Nancy -- and behind *him*.

Him. The man she had been married to for the past 22 years. The father of her two teenage daughters. *Him*.

She could see his mouth moving and realized that he had asked her something else.

"What?"

"Are you all right?" he repeated.

"I suppose so." She actually felt sort of shocky and numb.

Just then their waitress came by and asked if she wanted more coffee.

"Uh, sure." Nancy didn't really, but she was unable to think of anything else to say.

"I'll be right back with a fresh pot," the waitress responded before heading to the kitchen, popping her gum along the way and efficiently gathering empty plates as she passed vacated tables.

Nancy looked at Jonathon (*Him*) again and realized that he was watching her with an expression of sympathy on his face.

Suddenly she felt something more than just a hollow numbness; she felt something approaching irritation. Maybe even – YES – Anger.

How **dare** he pretend to care about her. How dare he feign compassion! For that matter, how dare he draw breath! She entertained a small fantasy about throwing her glass of water in his face and storming out of the restaurant, a la Katherine Hepburn. Then she took a deep breath and decided that maybe that wouldn't be prudent.

Not less than one minute ago (she was pretty sure it was only one minute) he had said that he thought it was time for them to split up.

Split up? As in divorce?

"Yes. I think that this is as good a time as any."

As good a time as compared to *when*?

Only an hour ago they had been looking at a new house to buy. Last week their 13 year old 'baby' arrived home from a two-week tour of China (of all places) with her karate team, which had left Nancy frantic with worry the whole time. Tomorrow Nancy's father was scheduled for an angiogram. And - oh yeah - two days ago she'd had another birthday. Of course . . . this just must be the perfect time.

Up until now, the few times in their marriage that Jonathon had talked about splitting up, Nancy had dragged him in for marriage counseling. Things would get better between them for a while and they'd be almost happy.

But right now, she just didn't have it in her to fight anymore.

"Why the hell not."

She wasn't truly angry ... not really. She was more confused than anything. Hadn't they just been looking at a new house with their realtor? Why would Jonathon have agreed to go house hunting if he wanted a divorce? They hadn't been fighting recently. In fact things had seemed to calm down a little. Then why the divorce?

"Babe, are you okay?"

Babe?

He'd called her "Babe?!?" This was getting more unreal by the moment.

"Yeah, I-I think so."

"You're crying."

"I am?"

"Yeah."

As she wiped her face with a napkin, the waitress stopped with fresh coffee. She looked at Nancy and then looked at Jonathon.

Jonathon shrugged his shoulders at the waitress and gave her a small 'women-what-can-you-do?' smile. The waitress frowned at him, her mouth diligently working the gum. The waitress' response actually felt kind of good; as though someone was on her side.

Sides. Oh, for pity's sake. Now there were going to be sides.

Jonathon pulled a folded sheet of paper out of his pocket and proceeded to read from it. "I've figured out what the child support should be. I'll also help with college for the girls. Of course I want final approval of which college they attend." He continued to talk in a normal tone.

College? Child support? Weren't they first supposed to talk about what had gone wrong? Wasn't there first supposed to be some sort of emotional catharsis?

Nancy's eyes moved around the restaurant again. Then it dawned on her. Of course! She looked back at Jonathon and realized that he had been afraid that she would become upset and there would be an argument. Hence, the restaurant instead of a private conversation. Apparently he thought that she wouldn't make a public display.

She sighed. He was right. He knew her pretty well after all.

"Why the hell not."

"So, it's okay with you?"

Not really. "Sure."

She held out her hand for the piece of paper that had been printed in his engineer-type block lettering, with evenly spaced columns and numbers. Good grief, he'd even put it in outline form! And now he wanted an answer. Nancy knew that she should get a lawyer. She knew that she should refuse to make any decisions at this time. She knew that she should take him for every penny she could get.

She also knew that she wouldn't do any of that. She just wasn't built that way. She even thought that maybe, somehow this was her fault. She was sure that if she'd only been thinner, younger, more athletic, more...well just more ANYTHING, this wouldn't be happening.

Didn't other marriages have rough patches? Didn't you stick

together through thick and thin? Weren't you supposed to honor in sickness and in health?

Obviously not everyone thought so.

Then Nancy had a thought that made her heart hurt.

"Is there someone else?" she asked haltingly.

"No." He seemed to be telling the truth. "Do you have someone else?"

What? What was he talking about? She wasn't the one asking for the divorce. He was. Unreal.

Jonathon went back to the figures on the paper and as he continued to talk about which items he wanted to keep and which she could have, her mind must have gone onto auto-pilot. Obviously, she agreed to many things because they were finished in about ten minutes.

Jonathon paid the bill, leaving a very small tip as usual, and for once Nancy didn't sneak a couple more dollars onto the table. For once she didn't even think about it. They moved towards the entrance doors just as two local police officers entered.

As Nancy walked past the officers, one of them turned to watch her walk by. He'd noticed her tear-streaked face and wondered what had happened to her.

Doug Saunders had entered the police force in order to help people and this woman sure looked like she could use some help. It had been a hell of a day for Doug, and he felt the need to be able to do something – anything – right. Just then a man about 5'10", thin and balding walked up behind the woman and escorted her out of the restaurant.

"Do you know her?" the other officer asked, looking back over his shoulder.

"No, Bill. She just seemed familiar somehow, that's all."

"Doug ol' buddy, that's the type of woman you should be dating. Not those bleached blond Balboa babes you hang out with." He gave Doug's shoulder a shove.

"My love life is off-limits as a topic of conversation." Doug placed his hat on the counter top, smiling at the waitress.

"Since when?" asked Bill, scooting onto the counter stool.

"Since now."

Grinning, Doug and his friend Bill picked up the menus and took sips of coffee from the mugs that the waitress had automatically placed before them. The image of the woman's tear-streaked face was filed into a back section of Doug's mind.

When Nancy and Jonathon exited the restaurant and walked out into the strong sunshine, Nancy was sure that she only had a few minutes left before she fell apart. She'd be damned if she'd let Jonathon see how much this had hurt. For some reason, right now pride was important.

"I have a few things to finish up in my classroom at the school. Could you just drop me off? I'll get a ride home." She was pretty sure that her voice didn't give anything away.

"Okay. Are you sure that you're all right?" He actually sounded as though he cared. *Yeah, right.*

The ride to the school was done in silence. Jonathon kept sneaking glances at Nancy, but couldn't read anything from her expression.

He dropped her off in front of her school, and Nancy walked to her classroom without looking back. Thank goodness no one else was around. She wasn't sure she had it in her to carry on a normal conversation right now.

She made it to her classroom unaccosted and locked the door behind her. Nancy slowly walked over to her desk on legs that felt as stiff and brittle as old wood. Measuring each step as she went, easing her way into the chair, she was afraid that if she moved any faster she'd crack. Moving slow seemed to be the glue that was holding her together right now, and if that's what it took to survive, then she'd move as slow as necessary.

She sat at her desk, resting her head in her hands, while her mind wandered over the past twenty-plus years, touching on various times, sort of like flipping through a photo album. Where had everything gone wrong?

Nancy remembered meeting Jonathon for the first time. She'd fallen in love with him when he'd directly asked her if she was already involved with someone. He'd seemed so sure of himself. When she'd said "No. No one." he'd then asked her if she was at all interested in him.

She'd thought that his directness indicated honesty. It had, but it had also indicated a lack of romance. However, she'd been swept off her feet so fast by his attention that she'd failed to notice the little things that were actually indicators of the bigger things.

Jonathon wasn't a mean man. He was just VERY practical. He didn't waste words. Such as "I love you." But if Nancy had been honest with herself, she would have realized that she was the type of woman who needed words. She also needed affection. And not just when Jonathon wanted to have sex. She needed to be told she was beautiful, or at least pretty. She remembered after she'd given birth to their second daughter and she'd looked up at him with joy. She expected him to tell her something like "thank you for the beautiful baby" or "you look radiant." Instead he'd told her that she needed to brush her hair.

And since Nancy was being honest with herself, she realized that he'd never once tried to convince her that he was anything other than what he was. She also realized that she'd harbored some sort of fantasy that he'd change his ways for her. When he didn't, she'd read that to mean that he didn't love her, which wasn't true.

She supposed he loved her in his own way. He'd provided well for her and the girls. He'd handled all the bills and their finances. He'd even purchased a new home for them. Jonathon would have fit in well back in the early 1950's. Too bad she wasn't Donna Reed.

Nancy actually hadn't wanted the kind of guy who was all emotional, and "in touch with his inner woman." She liked guys to be guys. She just hadn't wanted to feel like she was begging for attention and affection.

She wasn't sure how long she'd been sitting there, when the door was unlocked from the outside and her teacher's aide, Tess, walked in.

"How did the house-hunting go? Did you find the perfect place? I didn't expect to see you back here today." Tess hadn't even looked in Nancy's direction as she'd been talking a mile a minute. Instead she was dumping school supplies from her arms onto the nearest desk.

There were boxes of colored pencils, reams of lined paper, several pads of drawing paper, and a new 3-hole punch to replace the one that invariably got destroyed by one of the students every semester when they tried to punch too many pieces of paper at one time.

"How did Jonathon like the house? Did he like this one any better than the last one?" At that, Tess turned with a smile on her face to look at Nancy. In the space of a second, the smile vanished and was replaced with a small look of alarm.

"Are you all right?" Tess hurried to Nancy's side.

Nancy almost barked out a laugh. She had heard that question how many times in the last hour? She realized that Tess was truly concerned, but didn't have it in her just yet to explain what she'd been through. She wasn't even sure how she felt about it!

"I'm okay, Tess. I just ... have a migraine starting up." Nancy rubbed her right temple, as though it would make it seem like she really had a headache, and not a heartache.

"Why don't you go home, then? I'll take over for the day. In fact, take Monday off, too. All we have to do is get the classroom ready for the summer school crowd. I can do that by myself. We've already gone over the plans and I know what you want."

Nancy felt no qualms about leaving the classroom decor to Tess. In fact, Tess had brought fresh ideas with her when she came on board as a teacher's aide. Tess was natural as a teacher and Nancy counted herself lucky to have been chosen as Tess' mentor.

"I think you're right, Tess. Thanks. I'll go." Nancy picked up her purse, made sure she had her cell phone, and left. She got outside before she remembered that she didn't have her car.

Oh, for crying out loud! What next? She stood on the school sidewalk feeling the heat beat down on her shoulders while she debated her options. She didn't want to call Jonathon. She just couldn't face him yet. The girls were busy. They were home packing an overnight case to take with them to their grandparent's home. Dad!

That was just about Nancy's final undoing. Tomorrow was her dad's angiogram, and she had agreed to take him and Mom to the hospital. Nancy wavered on the emotional precipice of what could easily become an avalanche of self-pity.

From somewhere deep inside, Nancy shored up her reserves of

strength and decided that she'd just have to wait until later to fall apart. The divorce wasn't tomorrow. She didn't HAVE to move out just yet. Dad and the rest of her family came first right now. Okay, she was a performing arts teacher. Bring on Scarlett O'Hara. *I'll think about it tomorrow.*

Nancy took a deep breath, went back into the classroom and asked Tess if she'd mind terribly driving her home, because of her 'headache.'

Nancy felt bad about lying, but was determined to do whatever she had to do to get through the next few days. Not only for her parents' sake, but for her girls, too. The girls. How was she going to tell the girls?

Wait a minute. Hold on. It didn't have to happen now. No one needed to know right now. There was enough stress already with Dad's procedure. This could wait.

And wait it did while Nancy took care of her family.

Tess dropped her off in front of the house and Nancy thanked her for the umpteenth time.

"Give me a call!" Tess waved as she drove off.

Nancy took another deep breath. Well at least she was getting oxygenated today. A little giddy with overwhelm, Nancy mumbled under her breath, *"and, scene."* A small giggle erupted and Nancy clamped it down hard. It would be so easy to crumble here on the front porch and have a complete set of hysterics. Instead, she again pulled herself together, pasted a smile on her face and opened the front door.

"Girls! I'm home!" Nancy called out and instantly heard feet running upstairs.

Kate leaned over the upstairs banister and called down, "Hey, Mom! When did you want to leave?"

"Oh, we've got a couple of hours, honey. I haven't packed yet either. If we wait until after 5:00 we'll be able to miss the rush on the 91 freeway." Nancy was pleased with just how normal she sounded.

"Hey, Mom!" Christy's head appeared next to Kate's. "Is there room in the car for my skateboard and blades?"

"Of course, sweetie! If you want, we can even put the bike on the roof rack."

"Nah. We won't be there that long. Thanks anyways." Both Kate and Christy disappeared back into their rooms to finish packing.

Nancy wandered into the kitchen, the pristine white kitchen, and opened the refrigerator door. The chilled air felt good on her face. She removed a bottle of filtered water, found a glass and put ice cubes in it, then poured the water over the ice.

Taking the glass with her, Nancy moved into the pristine white living room and sat on the white leather couch.

Nancy actually would have loved more color in the house, but Jonathon wanted all white. He called it "minimal." She called it "boring." However, he'd always had the last say in the house décor, mainly because she didn't want to fight with him. She always felt like she'd lost a couple of IQ points after an argument with Jonathon. She thought something made perfect sense, but he'd convince her otherwise and by the end of the fight, her head was spinning.

Nancy sighed as she sipped on the water. Oh, well. Maybe after she got her own place she could spruce it up a bit. She'd definitely add more color and texture. And some pictures on the walls!

Jonathon only allowed pictures on one wall in the upstairs hallway.

However, Nancy had persevered and gotten Jonathon's agreement that the girls' rooms were theirs to do with as they wanted. His only stipulations were "no paint other than white" and "no nails."

So Nancy took the girls shopping and they found armfuls of posters that covered every square inch of wall space, attached by miles of tape.

The girls also had brightly colored bedspreads, pillows and throw rugs that accented the light beige Berber carpet that covered most of the floors in the house. The rest of the floors were done in light wood and white tiles. Clean, but uninspiring.

"When did I change?" Nancy tried to think back on if the change in her was subtle or if it happened overnight. Being a drama teacher, Nancy was anything but staid. For gosh sakes she used to belly dance at the Renaissance Faire! She loved color in her clothing and surroundings. She used to have tons of jewelry. Her ruby ring and pearl necklace used to be jumbled in her jewelry box right next to a huge assortment of costume jewelry. Nancy didn't care if the jewels were real or not. She bought jewelry if it was bright and artistic. Now her jewelry consisted of a pair of pearl and gold stud earrings, her wedding band, and her grandmother's ¼ carat diamond necklace. Much more in line with Jonathon's approval.

Her shoes had gotten more conservative, too. Nancy kept one pair of rhinestone studded ballroom dance shoes in the back of her closet and sometimes would pull them out and put them on just to see if they still fit. She'd given her ballet toe shoes to Kate and all the rest of her collection to the Goodwill when they'd moved into this house. Jonathon didn't want boxes and boxes of shoes cluttering the closet. Nevermind that they had separate closets and he didn't have to see inside Nancy's. "A cluttered house is a cluttered mind."

Big sigh. *Yes, I'm definitely getting more oxygen.*

Nancy finished her water and took the glass to the kitchen where she placed it in the top rack of the built in dishwasher. She took a paper towel and wiped down the counter – whether it needed it or not – and went upstairs to pack for her folk's house. She hoped she and the girls would be gone by the time Jonathon arrived home.

PAT ADEFF

CHAPTER 2

"It's only been one week and already I feel like the typical kid of a divorced family!" Kate exclaimed as she jumped into the front passenger seat of Nancy's 8-year old mini-van.

Nancy hid a grimace of guilt.

Their older girl, Kate was trying very hard to make the best of the situation. She sure wasn't happy about it, but seemed determined to not make it any more difficult for anyone else.

Jonathon had just pulled into the cobblestoned area in front of the gates at the guard station of their perfectly planned community in Irvine. He was coming home with Kate, and Nancy was taking off. She and the girls were going grocery shopping.

After dropping Kate, Jonathon drove past them into the gated community without even looking at Nancy, much less a wave or courteous comment.

Oh well, Nancy thought to herself. *Probably just as well*. She wasn't sure she could have been cordial. Her emotions had been on such a roller-coaster that sometimes she was surprised what came out of her mouth these days. Not to mention the thoughts that bounced around inside her head!

As Nancy pulled out of the gated area, she thought back seven years to when they had first moved here. Jonathon had purchased the second home available in the new community before it was even built. They'd stopped by regularly with the girls to see their house go up. They'd even made a time capsule with notes from each of them, a picture of the family, as well as a few trinkets from the girls, and placed it in one of the walls of the house before it had been finished. This had definitely been their ideal home. It was the perfect Orange County neighborhood.

That seemed like a lifetime ago. Now it seemed a little too *Stepford* for Nancy.

"Mom?"

"What?"

"I said, don't we have to pick up Christy? She's at Blake's."

"Oh, geez yes! Thanks, Hon. I almost forgot." Nancy made a quick left turn onto the next street.

"Mom? You okay?"

Good grief, the number of times she had heard that phrase over the past ten days.

She wanted to say *"No, not really. In fact I'm a basket case. I'm coming unglued at the seams and I just want to hit something*!" Actually not something -- someONE -- whose name began with a *J*!

Instead, she gave her daughter a smile and said "Yep. Just a little tired. Good thing I have you around to remind me." Nancy could tell from the look in Kate's eyes that she didn't believe her, but at least she didn't persist with more questions.

As Nancy and Kate drove over to Blake's house to get Christy, Nancy realized that she hadn't slowed down for one instant since Jonathon had asked for the divorce. She'd been there when her dad had come out of surgery and two days later she had been the one to drive him home and get him situated at her folk's house. Thank goodness the surgery had gone so well.

He'd sure given the family a scare, though. He'd never complained about anything. When he'd gone in for his angiogram, the doctor had treated the family like this was no big deal, and probably was all for nothing.

It wasn't until the doctor had come out of the room where he'd just finished the angiogram, looking slightly shaken but trying to hide it, that Nancy and her family knew that something was very wrong.

Her father had immediately been scheduled for heart surgery and had been transferred by ambulance over to St. Bernardine's Hospital, where the best heart surgeons were available for the triple bypass.

The next time her dad said he was feeling a little tired, the family was definitely going to pay closer attention.

Luckily, her dad was also a fast healer and was up in record time, giving the nurses a run for their money. *'There was this polar bear that walked into this bar...'*"

When they'd realized her dad needed heart surgery, she'd taken a short leave of absence from the school, and she and the girls had stayed in Redlands while her dad got back on his feet. But now that he was feeling better, her folk's house had seemed to grow smaller, and Nancy started feeling like they were in the way. So she and the girls headed home before they overstayed their welcome.

Home.

Not anymore. Now it just seemed like a house. A house with too many memories.

Time to move on.

That was it! They could sell the house and she and the girls could move right away. She and Jonathon had been looking for a new house anyway, so she'd just call the realtor and have her put their house on the market sooner than planned. Nancy felt slightly in charge of her life again – sort of.

As they pulled into Blake's driveway, Christy came running out the front door yelling "catch ya later" over her shoulder. She yanked open the door to the backseat, threw in her karate bag and jumped in behind it, slamming the door shut behind her.

"Hi, Mom!" Christy never seemed to do anything at less than full throttle. It always made Nancy smile. And for some weird reason, it always irritated Jonathon. Oh, well.

"Hi, sweetie! Have fun?"

"Yeah. We went down to the creek and caught some frogs."

"You didn't bring any in the car, did you?" Kate was half laughing, half serious.

"Nope. We let them go after one of them peed on Blake's hand."

"Oh, gross!" Kate was laughing hard.

"We're going shopping, want to come along?" Nancy laughed along with her two girls. They made everything she'd been going through worth it. Thank goodness, Jonathon was willing to let her have almost complete custody.

Looking around at the grocery store, it seemed to Nancy that the only people shopping except for her and the girls were couples. Young couples. Old couples. Middle age couples. Everyone was part of a couple except her. It made Nancy tired just trying to think about what had gone wrong with the marriage. She was so absorbed in her own thoughts, that she missed the look that passed between Kate and Christy. Then she had no more time to think when her girls started telling her about everything they'd done that day, in great detail and with much animation. They brought a smile to her face.

Later that afternoon, while Nancy was putting groceries away in the kitchen, Jonathon walked in from the garage, wiped his feet on the small mat at the back door and started to head upstairs to his home office.

"Jonathon. Do you have a minute?" Nancy was secretly pleased with herself at just how calm she sounded.

"Uh, sure."

He had been treading sort of lightly around Nancy. After getting back from her parents house, she'd made the living room couch into her bed. She supposed she should have made him sleep on the couch, but she just didn't want to have to put up with his complaining after his back was sure to go out if he wasn't able to sleep on his expensive "orthopedic" bed.

Over the years, they must have gone through six different beds in Jonathon's search for the perfect night's sleep.

She remembered how he'd insisted on using a waterbed during the time she was pregnant with Kate. She had tried explaining to him that she wasn't comfortable in the bed; that she just couldn't move easily because she couldn't get any sort of leverage to shift from one side to the other. However, Jonathon's back took precedence over her state of pregnancy and Nancy somehow made it through the pregnancy without too much difficulty. That was the first time she'd moved to the living room couch for any length of time.

Now Nancy watched him walk back to the kitchen area and sit tentatively on one of the barstools at the kitchen counter. He didn't seem to know what to do with his hands and after several uncomfortable attempts, finally settled on putting them on top of the counter in a loose grip.

Was it only a year ago that they'd gone shopping for those

barstools? Everything had seemed fine then. What had happened?

Nancy tried to suppress her sigh. She'd be damned if she'd let him see that she wasn't doing well.

"I was thinking that we should put the house on the market right away. I really don't want to stay here with the girls. We'll move closer to the school before the new school year starts." Nancy was pleased that her voice sounded pleasant. She felt slightly more in control.

'Um. I meant to tell you." Jonathon's eyes flitted everywhere but at Nancy.

"Meant to tell me what?" Okay. Good so far. Still sounded normal.

"I already, uh, called the real estate lady. She's coming over tonight to have us sign the papers to sell the house."

Nancy just stood there, a box of cereal in one hand and a bag of chips in the other, and stared at him. Just about the time she thought that she had pulled it all together, he broadsided her with something new. He'd already contacted the realtor without consulting with her. Typical Jonathon.

"Uh, okay." Nancy swallowed. "When is she due?" Forget trying to sound normal. Just get through this conversation.

"What time is it?" Jonathon looked around the kitchen as though he didn't know damn well where the clock was.

Nancy started to tell him the time, just like she'd always jumped whenever he'd asked for something throughout their whole married life. This time, though, he'd have to get it himself. In a split second some door inside of her soul slammed shut. It no longer mattered to her what Jonathon thought about her. It actually felt good to just stand there and make him do something for himself for once.

Jonathon waited, still stuck in the habits of the past. When he looked over at Nancy, waiting for her to tell him what time it was, he was stunned to find her humming and putting away the groceries! He wasn't upset, just surprised. Usually Nancy was pretty reliable in what she'd do.

"I think she might be due right now." His voice sounded smaller.

"Now? As in 6:00 o'clock?" Nancy frustration started to show in her expression and voice.

"Aw, come on, Nancy. Don't go getting all upset! You always do this! She's just coming over to sign some papers. It's no big deal. You always make such a big deal out of nothing." Jonathon had gone back to offense-mode.

Usually at this point in the conversation, Nancy would say that she wasn't upset, really. She'd apologize for her outburst, and then she'd try to move the conversation back into safer waters.

This time, however, she didn't care. She ignored him while she finished putting away the groceries and started dinner. Okay, okay, so she slammed some cupboards while doing it. Grilled chicken, fresh veggies, potatoes, but no rice - Jonathon was allergic to rice, unless his mother made it - and a tossed salad. Nancy smiled to herself as she hand-shredded the lettuce – imagining each piece was a piece of Jonathon.

What the heck, Nancy added a pot of rice. She supposed that some TV guru would say that she was being "passive-aggressive" but she just didn't care. The simple truth was that she and the girls liked rice. She just never made it for dinner because Jonathon made such a big fuss over the fact that he was allergic to it. He didn't swell up or get hives or anything that drastic. He just had digestion problems. No one was forcing it down his throat. He didn't have to eat the rice.

Nancy set an extra plate at the table. If the real estate lady showed up during dinner time, she'd probably be hungry. There was no sense in stopping dinner just for business.

At some point while Nancy was cooking, Jonathon must have wandered off to his computer. It felt good to not feel that she had to answer to him. There was a new feeling of freedom in it.

In fact, Nancy was feeling so perky that she went into the garage and found their old am/fm radio, brought it into the kitchen and tuned in a 1940's swing station. Dinner was easy to cook while humming along with Benny Goodman.

The lady showed up, papers in hand, at 7:00 o'clock.

"Please join us for dinner. There's plenty." Nancy was actually glad to have someone else at the dinner table.

To Nancy's surprise, the woman accepted. She smiled and said that she hadn't eaten anything since lunch and was starving. As the meal progressed, Nancy and the girls had a wonderful conversation with the realtor. Nancy could tell that Jonathon was becoming disgruntled because they were wasting time with what he called "chitchat." And for once, she didn't try to soothe him.

Finally, the real estate lady finished dinner as well as the conversation they were having, and handed Jonathon the papers to sign.

"Why are you selling?" the woman said while looking in her briefcase for a pen. She finally looked up when her question was met with silence. She looked over at Nancy. Nancy was stunned to learn that Jonathon hadn't said anything to the lady.

"We're getting a divorce." Jonathon's voice seemed almost sincerely sad. Nancy couldn't believe that he was trying to make it sound as though this was a mutually agreed upon decision!

"Jonathon asked for a divorce a couple of weeks ago." Nancy tried to keep her voice neutral. For some reason it was important to Nancy that it be known that Jonathon had wanted the divorce, not her.

The lady paused, looking between Nancy and Jonathon's faces, trying to decipher the tone of conversation. Nancy took pity on her and moved along with the papers.

The rest of dinner felt odd and stifled. The girls became unusually quiet. No more stories of the exploits of that day graced the dinner table. Nancy and the woman haltingly discussed the new Mayor and his daughter's latest escapade with the local authorities.

When the front door was finally closed after all papers had been signed in what seemed like ten copies each, Nancy went to the kitchen and started doing dishes after she sent the girls off to get ready for bed.

Jonathon came into the kitchen as she was loading the dishwasher, and leaned against one of the counters. She had to move around him to get some of the dirty pots and pans from the stove.

He just leaned there, not helping as usual, with his arms crossed.

"Do you want to talk?"

"No, not really." Nancy was rinsing out the glasses before putting them into the top rack.

"Well, then what was that all about?" Jonathon sounded edgy.

"What was what all about?" Nancy pushed in the top rack and pulled out the bottom rack for the plates.

"Will you stop that and look at me?" Now he just sounded mad.

"Actually, no I won't. You see, usually after one of these types of conversations, you go to bed, and I am up late finishing the dishes, getting lunches ready for tomorrow and getting one last load of laundry done. Tonight, I'm going to get enough sleep. If you want to talk, we'll do it tomorrow after work." With that said, Nancy went back to putting plates and pots in the bottom rack of the dishwasher. She wasn't sure exactly when Jonathon left the kitchen.

When her head finally hit her pillow, Nancy felt almost good. For the first time in a long time, she slept throughout the whole night and woke up feeling rested.

In fact, she felt so energized that over the weekend she painted the downstairs guest bathroom a soft sage green and added some pretty ecru lace towels she found on sale. Then she went to the new little downtown boutique and picked up some pink rose-scented bars of soap and a small container of potpourri.

Their realtor was delighted with the bathroom and asked Nancy to do the upstairs one as well. She felt the value of the house would go up with the improved décor. The only reason Jonathon did not voice any disapproval this time, was because he liked the idea of more money for the house.

And so life continued for the next several weeks.

CHAPTER 3

"Menopause!?!"

Dr. Worksley looked up from Nancy's patient folder where she'd been studying the lab results.

"No, not menopause. Perimenopause. Does that bother you, Nancy?"

Dr. Worksley was an excellent doctor. Nancy had found her two years before the divorce when Jonathon's health plan from work was switched ... again.

"No. I'm just surprised. That's all." Nancy lifted one shoulder and tried to appear composed, while sitting on the hard examining table wearing nothing more than thin paper. Perimenopause. Well, that pretty much put the icing on the cake. Could her life get any more complicated?

After receiving the usual advice of "get more sleep, cut down on sugar and coffee, and try to fit in some time for exercise," Nancy was released from her yearly physical.

She'd declined Dr. Worksley's offer of a prescription for hormone replacement drugs. Nancy thought she'd wait a bit to see what was going to happen before taking a pill. This certainly explained the occasional hot flash and her inability to sleep through the night.

After getting dressed, Nancy stopped by the front desk and paid her co-pay. She only had two more years on Jonathon's health plan according to the divorce agreement. She had no idea what she would do after that. The private school where she worked didn't offer medical benefits.

Driving back to work, Nancy had time to contemplate where her life was going now that she and the girls were living by themselves.

Jonathon had managed to land at one of the newer singles apartment complexes, complete with pool, spa, outdoor barbecue, gym room and a gaggle of firm, attractive 20-somethings.

Nancy and the girls were renting a house close to the school. The house was old and the landlord was slightly creepy. However, the neighborhood was wonderful and their neighbors were happy to have a nice normal woman and her nice normal children living there. Apparently the previous tenants hadn't fit in very well with the family-based neighborhood. The girls each had their own bedroom and Nancy even had room for an office! Unfortunately most of her office stuff was still in boxes, but at least there was no one to complain to her about it.

It had been three months since the split. Three months that had produced some interesting results. Jonathon was already dating someone. He sure hadn't wasted any time. Whereas, Nancy had decided that her girls came first. Besides, she just wasn't in the mood to date. She was enjoying not being criticized 24/7. So she had made the conscious decision to wait until the girls were out on their own to throw her hat back in the dating pool – ring – whatever.

Jonathon had joined an adult volleyball team, a Tai Chi group in Newport Beach, a fencing class that he'd talked Kate into attending with him, not to mention the bicycling club that Nancy personally thought was ridiculous. He looked awful in the spandex outfits they wore. When had she ever thought Jonathon attractive?

Nancy had also been busy during those three months.

She'd purchase her first car, gotten a new queen-size bed that she thought was extravagant, gained 12 pounds (not on purpose) and during one glorious pity-party had burned all of her wedding pictures.

Kate and Christy seemed to be hanging in there despite the stress of the split. Kate had even gone to her first prom, which could have gone smoother. Jonathon was supposed to drive Kate and her date to the dance but was late picking her up, which of course put Kate in a bad mood, which made her date nervous, which made for five days of very uncomfortable living around the house for Nancy and Christy after what came to be known as the *Prom Fiasco*.

When Nancy asked about his tardiness, Jonathon casually said that he'd had to work.

When Nancy asked why he hadn't called to say he was running late, Jonathon told her to stop making it into such a big deal. Nancy sighed and decided that she'd just drive from now on. It was so much easier than trying to work with Jonathon.

Between the two girls, Christy seemed to be doing better. One evening after supper, she told Nancy that she was glad they weren't living with dad anymore. Nancy asked her why. Christy replied that she liked not getting yelled at all the time.

Perplexed, Nancy asked more questions, and Kate jumped into the conversation too. Apparently, Jonathon would wait until Nancy had left to run errands before he'd start in on the girls. It seemed that pretty much nothing they did was good enough. He'd nag, badger or yell about whatever he felt needed correction. The girls were surprised to find out that Nancy had known nothing about it! They thought she knew that Jonathon did this.

Nancy felt betrayed. She also felt like a very bad mother, leaving her girls at the mercy of that sort of behavior.

Of all the stories Nancy heard that night, one was the worst and made her sick. Nancy knew about it somewhat, but not to the extent that the girls were now telling her.

It had happened about 10 years earlier...

Nancy remembered being happy that Jonathon had agreed to watch the girls so that she could go to the movies with one of her friends that Saturday afternoon.

She and her friend Brenda both had children the same age, so they rarely got a chance to talk without the constant interruption that is typical around young children.

They'd gone to see the new Kevin Costner movie and then gone for coffee. It had been a wonderfully relaxing afternoon for Nancy. For the first time in a long time, she'd felt like someone who was more than just "mother."

When she got back to the house, she found Jonathon in the kitchen reading the newspaper and having coffee. She found the girls sitting on the living room couch watching TV. On the surface it all looked calm, but Nancy felt something was amiss.

"So. How'd it go around here?" she asked Jonathon while taking off her jacket and setting down her purse and keys.

He looked up from the paper and said "Actually, it's been pretty quiet. I don't know what you complain about. The girls aren't hard to deal with."

"I've never said that the girls are hard to deal with!" Nancy was puzzled that Jonathon thought that.

"Well then, what do you keep complaining about?" Now it was Jonathon's turn to look puzzled.

"What are you talking about? When have I complained?"

"Just yesterday! You said that you never got any time to yourself. That's why I baby-sat today."

"Baby-sat!? They're your children. You're *supposed* to spend time with them."

"There! That's what I'm talking about. You're complaining again!"

"Jonathon, I don't want to argue! I had a great afternoon with Brenda and now in the space of two minutes ... oh, never mind." Nancy went upstairs to change her clothes.

When she came back downstairs a few minutes later, the girls were still on the couch watching TV. Nancy went to the couch and sat down between the girls, putting an arm around each of them. They both cuddled close to her and the three of them sat there watching Big Bird sing to Oscar the Grouch.

When the show was over Nancy got up and shut off the set. She turned back to the girls and asked if they wanted to help set the table for dinner. It was then, while really looking at them, Nancy saw that they looked devastated. They both had hollow-looking eyes and not much color in their faces. There were old tear tracks running down Christy's cheeks.

"What happened?" Nancy softly asked as she knelt down in front of the couch so she'd be at eye level with the girls.

"I hate Daddy."

Nancy couldn't have been more shocked! Christy had said it with such vehemence! Nancy then looked at Kate. Kate was starting to quietly cry.

"Girls! What happened?"

Neither was willing to say anything more. Nancy got up, told the girls to wait there and went into the kitchen. Jonathon was still reading the newspaper and drinking his coffee.

"What happened here this afternoon?"

"Why? What do you mean?" Jonathon actually looked almost blank.

"The girls are upset. What happened?"

"Oh, nothing really. They threw away their baby bottles." He went back to sipping his coffee.

"Why'd they do that?"

"Because they are getting too big for bottles."

"Jonathon. They don't really drink out of them anymore. They just play with them. Very rarely, Christy likes one at bedtime if it's been a really rough day. You didn't *make* them throw their bottles away, did you?"

"Look, Nancy. I think you're being too soft with the girls. They are big girls now and need to get rid of all their baby stuff. You keep bitching at me that I'm not being a dad, now you're bitching at me because I'm parenting. Make up your mind."

Nancy felt sick. She went back into the living room and sat down with the girls. After some more questions, it came out that not only had Jonathon made the girls physically throw the bottles away while they were crying, but he made them "wave bye-bye" to the bottles.

He had explained to the girls that it was kind of like the funeral they'd had the week before when their pet hamster had died. Nancy couldn't fathom how Jonathon thought that particular correlation could possibly help.

She wasn't sure what to do at this point, but knew for sure that her girls were hungry. She stood up and got them to go wash their hands for dinner.

Everyone sat quietly around the table while Nancy served up the chicken and dumpling dinner that she'd started earlier that day in the crock-pot. She added a salad from the fridge and pudding cups for dessert.

Kate and Christy ate a little, Nancy ate even less and Jonathon ate as usual. When dinner was done, Nancy took the girls upstairs and got them into bed. By the time she was done with that, Jonathon was buried in the computer, so she cleaned up the kitchen and got things set up for the next day's breakfast.

Now it was ten years later, and Nancy was hearing these things again, but seeing them in a new light.

"Girls. I'm sorry. I should have made sure you didn't have to go through anything like that. I guess I just didn't believe that your father would actually be that callous." Nancy's voice was choked with unshed tears.

"Aw, Mom. Lighten up. We lived. Besides, we know you pretended not to notice when we each retrieved a bottle out of the trash bag they were in." Kate was almost laughing.

"Yeah! And remember when you pretended to not see the bottles when we put them in the dishwasher?" Christy was also laughing.

Nancy was able to smile slightly. "So, whatever happened to the bottles?"

Both girls jumped up off the couch and ran to their respective rooms. Within seconds they were both back, laughing and holding out their bottles.

"Good grief! I always wondered what you did with them." Nancy was feeling much better now.

"Mom," said Kate. "You are a good mom. Please don't worry anymore!"

"Yeah, Mom," chimed in Christy. "Consider it as training for the type of guy that Kate and I AREN'T going to look for!"

"Girls, your father is a good man. He just --"

Nancy was cut off mid-sentence by the girls, "Mom! Stop already!"

Laughing, Nancy said "All right. Anyone interested in ice cream?"

The girls were up and racing for the front door. Kate grabbed the car keys as Christy grabbed the latest coupons from the table beside the front door. The ice cream parlor was only a two minute drive.

"You just want to see Brett," Christy was taunting Kate.

"I do not!" Kate was unable to suppress her grin.

As Nancy followed the girls to the car, she smiled and sighed. Yep, life was going to turn out all right after all.

She had the girls. She had her health. She had a great job. Who needed a man? Nancy didn't really want to take that thought any further. She knew lots of women who lived great lives without a man. But for some reason, she just couldn't remember who they were right then.

When they got to the ice cream parlor, the girls and Nancy had a hard time deciding which ice cream combinations they wanted. Nancy had trouble deciding because she really wanted to lose a couple of pounds, yet she really REALLY wanted some chocolate. So she ordered the kid size cup as a compromise.

Christy finally ordered what she wanted – French vanilla with crushed Butterfinger candy.

However, Kate was having a heck of a time deciding, so Brett (bless his heart) took the time to make sure she tasted every single one of the flavors.

Nancy and Christy took their cups of delight and by silent agreement went outside to sit at one of the benches. When Kate finally appeared, they'd finished and were waiting patiently.

The drive home consisted of Christy asking twenty questions about Brett, and Kate fielding the questions like a seasoned politician. Nancy loved the fact that the girls were intelligent and witty. Intelligence from their dad and witty from her. She smiled to herself. Witty beat intelligence any day of the week.

PAT ADEFF

CHAPTER 4

The top of her birthday cake looked like a forest fire.

Nancy was laughing on the outside but cringing inwardly. Was she really that old now? She didn't feel that old. In fact, her life's theme song was Bryan Adam's *Eighteen 'til I Die*.

She'd just finished blowing out all the candles from her surprise birthday cake. The girls had somehow managed to fill their house with friends in the fifteen minutes it had taken Nancy to run to the store earlier that afternoon for a gallon of milk that the girls "just had to have."

"Where's the fire extinguisher?" joked Christy's boyfriend, Jackson.

"Forget the extinguisher! Where's the firemen!" chimed in Kate.

The guests laughed and poked fun at Nancy. They all knew the soft spot she had in her heart for firefighters and cops. To Nancy, these guys were true heroes. Because her uncle had been the Fire Chief for Crestline, Nancy had grown up around firefighters, cops and EMTs and she'd admired them all her life.

As the afternoon turned to early evening, the guests left one-by-one until it was just Christy and Jackson, and Kate and her current boyfriend, Joey.

Nancy could hardly believe that four years had passed since the divorce.

"Hey, Mom." Kate was getting her purse and sweater. "We're

going to the movies. Wanna come?"

Nancy wanted to go, but being a fifth-wheel just seemed too much. "No. You go ahead and have fun. I've got some things I'd like to do around here."

"You're sure?" Christy was grabbing her motorcycle helmet and jacket.

"Yep. I'm sure. But thanks for asking!"

Standing in the front doorway, Nancy watched the girls leave with their boyfriends and was once again struck with how beautiful they'd grown up to be. They'd also managed to find good men. Obviously a trait Nancy was lacking. Sighing, she decided to keep busy. No need to go there.

First Nancy looked through the basket of clothes that needed mending. Sigh. Later. Next she pulled out all the paperwork for paying bills. Tomorrow. She even opened the oven door to see how much work it would be to clean. Forget it.

She finally decided to treat herself and watch a movie at home. She picked out a Keanu Reeves flick and settled down with a bowl of popcorn and a cup of herb tea. The movie had just gotten to Nancy's favorite part where Keanu's character falls in love with an older woman, when the phone rang.

With her eyes on the TV screen, she picked up the phone and answered. "Hello?" Nancy was expecting her dad and mom to call and wish her Happy Birthday. Instead she heard crying.

"M-mom?" Kate was trying to stay calm, but Nancy could hear the panic through the tears.

"Honey? What's happened?" Nancy sat up straight on the couch. Her insides were drawing tight and it was becoming hard to breath.

"Mom..." Kate's breath hitched and she let out a sob. "Mom, we were in an accident."

"Where are you?" Nancy was on her feet, trying not to think about the worst that could happen. "HOW are you?"

"Oh, Mom. We didn't see the truck. It just came out of *nowhere!*" Nancy could hear voices and traffic noise in the background. She heard a man's voice and Kate's cell phone switching from one hand to another.

"Mrs. Adams?" a male voice asked.

"Yes. This is Nancy Adams. Please tell me what's happened. Is anyone hurt?"

"Mrs. Adams. This is Officer Saunders of the Orange Police Department. Can you meet us at Memorial Hospital? That's where the paramedics are taking her."

"Kate? Kate's going to the hospital?"

"No ma'am. It's Christina. They're taking her and Jackson to Memorial. Do you know how to get there?"

"How bad is it? Are they...are they still alive?"

"Ma'am, do you need me to send a car for you?"

Oh, god. He won't even say if she's alive! "No. I'll drive. Please let me talk to Kate again."

Once again the phone switched hands.

"Mom? Are you coming?"

"Kate? How bad is it really?" Nancy readied herself for the worst.

"I don't know. There's blood everywhere and Christy's already gone in an ambulance. Jackson is still here. He's moving, so he's at least alive. Oh Mom!" Kate's voice sobbed again.

"Honey, please let me talk to Joey." Nancy tried to keep her voice somewhat level. She heard the phone change hands again.

"Uh, hi, Mrs. Adams." Joey's voice cracked and sounded much younger than his 20 years.

"Joseph. I need you to get Kate in the car and follow Jackson's ambulance to the hospital. I'll get there as soon as I can. And drive carefully!"

"Okay. The ambulance is pulling out right now. We'll see you at the hospital."

And with that, the line went dead.

As she placed the receiver back in the phone cradle, Nancy started to feel fingers of panic plucking at her spine and stomach, and almost gave in to the roiling emotion.

NO! Through sheer determination, she stopped and pulled her thoughts together. She grabbed the insurance cards off the dresser, her purse, cell phone and car keys and headed out the door.

As she was backing out of the driveway, she kept thinking "Everything's going to be all right. Everything's going to be all right." It was the mantra that got her through the evening traffic and to the hospital. Although the traffic was not particularly heavy, it seemed to Nancy that she was driving in slow motion and that it took forever to arrive.

CHAPTER 5

As Nancy flew through the sliding doors into the Emergency Room waiting area, she was assaulted by the smell of disinfectant with the underlying tang of injured flesh and vomit.

The place was packed and noisy. All the chairs were filled, and people were standing along the walls and in the corners. There were several couples, young and old, a few families, a flock of worried cheerleaders, and a baby crying in pain. Usually Nancy would have paid attention to the baby and the mother holding and rocking her child. However, one of HER babies was behind the double doors leading into the treatment area of the ER, and she needed to get there - NOW.

She spied the ER admitting desk. Navigating through the injured and ill, she rushed over to the line of people waiting to check in. Nancy was feeling the panic start to bubble out, and just about the time she decided to be very rude and cut in front of everyone, the double doors to her right opened up.

"Mom! Over here." Kate and Joey had been on the lookout for her.

Nancy hurried over to them and after giving Kate a swift hard hug, and checking to make sure she was okay, they led her inside and down the corridor, walking rapidly towards the two end units. Lining the hall were gurneys with patients in various stages of pain. One of the beds held a frail older woman who was plucking at her blanket while whispering "Please" over and over in an eerie voice. An EMT stood at the foot of the woman's bed, writing notes on a clipboard. Another bed had a teenage boy in a football uniform holding his left elbow with his right hand. Behind the sweat and messy hair in his face, Nancy could see the fear and the tears he was valiantly trying to hold back. Well, that explained the contingent of cheerleaders in the waiting room.

They finally made it to the end of the hall. At the first curtain, Nancy peeked around and saw Jackson sitting up with his eyes closed and a nurse checking his blood pressure. Jackson looked pale and exhausted. He had a wide bandage around his rib area. The nurse nodded and smiled at Nancy to indicate that he was alright.

Nancy smiled back and then moved to the next curtain. Taking a deep breath she pushed the curtain aside.

Nothing.

The bed was empty. There were bloody dressings scattered on the counter and floor. There was blood on the rumpled sheet on the bed.

She couldn't breathe. Where was Christy? Why was there so much blood!? Nancy was looking around to find someone to answer her questions when she heard a faint "Mom?"

Being pushed down the corridor, sitting on a gurney with a huge white bandage around her head was Christy.

"Mom!" Christy held out her hand and Nancy's feet finally started to move.

"Oh, honey. Are you all right? What happened?" Nancy gripped Christy's hand like a vise between both of hers.

"Mom! Ease up. I'm OK." Christy even managed a watery half-smile. She held up the hand that Nancy was squeezing in two.

"Oh, honey. I'm sorry. I'm just so glad to see you're alive." Nancy loosened her grip a little, but not much. "What happened to you? There's so much blood!"

"That's from her head wound. She took twelve stitches." The doctor came around from behind Christy's gurney and helped the orderly maneuver the bed back into place in the cubicle.

Nancy mentally shook her head. The doctor looked no older than her daughter, Kate. It seemed to her that all doctors and dentists were getting younger and younger these days.

"Head wounds are notorious for producing copious amounts of blood," Dr. Derek Coburn explained, then said to the orderly, "Let's get this cleaned up."

The orderly seemed to magically take all the bloody material with him when he left the unit, pushing the other gurney away to the back of the ER. Except for a little spot of dried blood on the gown that Christie was wearing, everything looked clean.

"Jackson? How are you, babe?" Christy called to him through the curtain.

No answer.

"Jackson?" Christy swung her feet around as though she intended to get out of bed.

"Whoa there little lady." Dr. Coburn gently pushed Christy's feet back on the bed. "Just a second." He smiled at Kate as she moved to stand on the other side of Christy's bed.

The doctor stuck his head around the curtain separating the two units. He said something to the nurse, listened, and then turned around and smiled at Christy while he pushed back the curtain which separated the two areas.

Sitting up in bed was Jackson with huge round eyes. "Babe? You OK?"

He started to get up and the nurse put a restraining hand on his shoulder. "Easy there. She's all right. See? Alive and breathing."

Christy and Jackson eye's both filled with tears as they looked at each other, realizing how close they'd come to losing everything.

Nancy looked around and saw Kate's eyes filled with tears, too. Joey was valiantly trying to look unmoved; however his own eyes looked pink.

"Well, we're a sorry bunch." Nancy wiped at her own eyes and tried to smile a watery smile at the group. She turned to the doctor.

"So, how badly were they beat up?"

"We should get the x-ray results back in a few minutes. I'll let you know as soon as I know." He handed Kate a tissue, squeezed Nancy's shoulder reassuringly and walked over to the nurse's station to write something in a chart.

"Okay. So now we wait." Nancy took a seat in one of chairs between the gurneys and looked around at everyone. "What happened?"

The four of them started talking all at once. Nancy was able to get from snatches of what they were saying that a truck had run a red light and was going to crash into Jackson's motorcycle from the side. Luckily Jackson had been paying attention. When he saw the truck coming at them, he sped up so that the truck just bumped the back fender of the bike, sending it up and over the curb where the two of them went sky-born.

Christy's head laceration happened after she'd gotten up, taken off her helmet and slipped on a patch of oil, hitting her head on a broken piece of concrete on the side of the road. Jackson had ended up with a bruised rib cage where he'd hit the handlebars as he flew over them. Thank goodness nothing worse happened.

"What about the truck driver?" Nancy looked at Kate.

"I think the police took him away."

"Was he under the influence?"

"We don't know."

"How old was he?"

"I think around my age," Joey chimed in.

Several minutes passed with only small talk happening. In the background there were the haunting sounds of machines beeping, soft crying, and murmuring voices. Punctuating this background noise was the occasional grunt or groan of pain. Dr. Coburn came back holding the x-rays, and gave both Jackson and Christy clean bills of health, telling Christy to make an appointment to have the stitches removed in about a week.

As the doctor spoke, he pulled out a deck of cards from his pocket. Glances were exchanged all around while they waited to see what the doctor was going to do.

"Do we each pick a card and high card pays the ER bill?" Kate teased the doctor.

His eyes cut to Kate and a mysterious smile appeared on his lips. "No, but that's an interesting idea. No, I just wanted to show you something."

Then Dr. Derek Coburn, ER doctor extraordinaire, did something that Nancy had never seen a doctor do before. He did magic without the use of needles, drugs or x-rays. He proceeded to charm everyone into smiling by doing a feat of magic wherein he had Kate pick a card and write her phone number on it. Then he made the card disappear, only to reappear under the battery in her cell phone! It was phenomenal.

Once Kate had examined the card in wonder and declared it was her original card, Dr. Coburn put the card in his pocket and returned to business.

He handed all the follow-up papers to Kate and also handed her what appeared to be his business card. Nancy was shaking her head in wonderment while she came to her feet.

Everyone gathered up their belongings and left the hospital after Nancy dealt with the admittance desk and gave the hospital the insurance information. Christy and Jackson were put in the backseat of Nancy's car, while Kate and Joey followed them to the house in his car.

Arriving home, they walked into the living room where the bowl of popcorn had been upended all over the carpet and the tea cup was on its side with a small wet stain next to it. The four young people looked at Nancy and she glanced back awkwardly.

"I guess I was a little excited when I got your call. I'll clean it up."

"Nope, Mom. You sit down with Christy and Jackson. Joey and I'll get it." Kate was in charge for the moment. It felt good to have someone else giving the orders for a while. Nancy sank wearily onto the couch and counted her blessings while she gathered in her kids.

She thought of calling Jonathon, but realized that all he'd do was ask her twenty questions and tell her everything she'd done wrong. She wasn't in the mood right now. She'd call him tomorrow and let him know how everyone was doing.

Maybe.

CHAPTER 6

"Just a minute!" Nancy shouted to whoever had just knocked at the front door. She closed the dishwasher door and was wiping her hands with a kitchen towel when she opened the door.

Then she just stared.

Broad navy-blue shoulders filled her field of vision.

Mirrored sunglasses glinted in the sunlight.

The badge flashed as strong hands reached up to pull off sunglasses.

Dark blue, almost obsidian eyes crinkled at the corners as he smiled. The eyes cut to Nancy's hand where the kitchen towel had just slipped from her fingers and fallen to the ground.

Nancy felt mortified by her reaction. She pulled herself out of whatever spell she'd fallen under and reached down for the towel at the same time the officer reached down. They ended up bumping shoulders. Nancy started to fall sideways but was stopped when she felt strong warm hands grab her shoulders and help her stand upright.

Feeling her face flush (another hot flash, thank you!) she reached up to sweep the hair out of her face. "Oh, I'm sorry," she breathed out.

"Not a problem. Are you all right?" He removed his hands from her shoulders and she suddenly wished he hadn't. Then reality took over and she realized that she'd been staring at the Kevlar vest covering his chest. She shot her eyes back up to his and watched his gaze warm.

"Here, let me." He bent over and picked up the kitchen towel, handing it to her.

"Thank you." She managed a smile, but lost it as soon as she realized that this was a police officer at her door.

"The kids..." she started with a worried look.

"They're fine. At least as far as I know." He hooked the sunglasses onto his shirt pocket. "I'm Officer Saunders. Doug Saunders."

Nancy just looked at him blankly. (Okay, and perhaps sort of dreamily too.)

"I was the officer who talked to you over the phone from the site of your daughter's motorcycle accident last week." He seemed to grow younger before her eyes.

"Oh! Yes, of course. Sorry about that. I didn't recognize your voice. Although we only spoke for a few minutes. Actually it was just a few seconds, not minutes. And it was over a cell phone. Thank you for helping them. How are you?" *Shut up Nancy. You're babbling.*

"I'm fine. How are you doing?" His killer smile made him look like a kid.

"Oh, um. I'm fine. Thank you for asking. How are you?"

Grinning he replied. "I'm still fine."

Nancy realized that she was acting like a complete idiot. Then it dawned on her that she was wearing her rattiest tee-shirt, cut-offs and tennies. Her "cleaning house" outfit. Yep, faded navy tee-shirt, tan sagging cut-offs, and old white tennies which were filthy. Not to mention no make-up and her hair flying everywhere.

She was very aware of the difference between her unfashionable attire and the officer's precisely creased uniform.

Then she chastised herself. This man wasn't there to flirt with her. Did she really think that real life was like the movies? He probably wasn't even there to see her. He needed to see Jackson and Christy. Yes, that must be it.

"They won't be back for a while." She managed to pull herself together.

"Who?" He genuinely looked puzzled.

"The kids. That's who you're here for. Right?"

"No. I'm not. I need to give you some information and find out what you want to do about it."

Okay. The conversation had now gone into left field and Nancy was clueless about what he was talking about.

"You're looking for me?"

"You're Mrs. Adams, right?"

"Mrs. Adams is my ex-mother-in-law. I'm Nancy." Nancy winced and suddenly hated how the witticism she'd used ever since the divorce now sounded a little bitter. Wiping the towel across her forehead, she managed a small smile, "Sorry. An old joke, beyond its expiration date."

He smiled back.

"May I come in?"

"Oh! Of course. I've been keeping you out here in the hot sun. What was I thinking? Of course, come in."

She stepped back into the entry hall and he followed her inside, filling the small entry space and emptying it of all oxygen.

"Would you like some iced tea? Coffee?" Nancy indicated to him to have a seat in the living room as she turned left into the kitchen to retrieve beverages … and breath.

"I said would you like...*whoof!*" When she hadn't gotten an answer, she had reversed direction to call into the living room and had suddenly run into a wall. A warm, masculine, broad-shouldered wall. Armored in Kevlar.

Once again, warm hands wrapped around her shoulders as she gained her footing.

"I can't believe I'm doing this! I am so sorry. I don't know what's gotten into me." Nancy swiftly stepped back as he dropped his hands. Again a feeling of bereftment. She was starting to realize exactly how long it had been since she'd been close to an adult male. ANY adult male.

"Coffee? Tea?" She almost giggled as she squelched the urge to say "Me?"

For heaven's sake! What HAD gotten into her?

"Coffee. If it's no trouble." He leaned his hip against the counter next to the coffee pot and adjusted the volume on his radio, while he spoke into his lapel mike. As his lips moved, Nancy noticed how nicely chiseled they were. Then she noticed that his eyes were watching her looking at his mouth.

Nancy spun around to the sink so fast, her hair went even wilder than it was before. She studiously filled the pot with water, put a new filter and grounds into the coffee maker and pushed the button, while he finished speaking with the police dispatcher.

Nancy was extremely aware of his proximity, and took a step back before looking up into his face.

He didn't seem to be affected in the least. Well, of course not. He was here on official business and was probably much younger than her.

Oh well, the fantasy was fun.

"So. What can I help you with?" Nancy was all business as she led him into the living room to wait for the coffee. If she had seen the way his eyes traveled from her neck to her heels and back up again, and his small suppressed smile, she would have realized that maybe he wasn't feeling entirely businesslike.

As they sat at opposite ends of the couch, he pulled out a small notepad and flipped through the pages looking for his notes. Nancy admired how masculine and strong his hands were. *Well!* she thought. *I guess I'm not dead yet.*

Officer Saunders looked up and his eyes met Nancy's.

Just as he started to speak, the front door burst open with the girls and Jackson and Joey right behind them.

"Mom? You okay?" Both Kate and Christy wore concerned looks on their faces. "We saw the police car out front."

Officer Saunders rose and shook hands with the girls. "Hi, I'm Doug Saunders. I just came by to ask your mom some questions."

"Oh! I remember you. You were at the accident." Kate said.

"Oh, yeah! Thank you for your help." Jackson also reached out and shook hands with the officer. Joey just stood there with his hands in his pockets.

Everyone else relaxed. "Can we join you?" Kate set her backpack down on the floor.

Nancy turned to the officer and raised her eyebrows in question. He smiled at Nancy, nodding his approval and everyone sat down. Nancy looked over in time to see Christy and Kate share a look. She frowned at them and they both turned blank faces to her, as though the look had not happened.

Just then the coffee pot beeped that the coffee was done.

Nancy jumped up. "What do you take in it?"

"Just black if it's good, but lots of cream and sugar if it's not." Officer Saunders had a sense of humor.

"Oh, it's good. I'm actually very good in the kitchen." Nancy suddenly turned and fled into the kitchen. She couldn't believe that she'd just said that. It sounded like she was trying to be suggestive. She wasn't! It just popped out of her mouth.

When she came back into the living room with two cups of coffee, Officer Saunders and the kids were laughing over something.

Doug stood up and took the coffee cup from Nancy's hand, took a sip and sighed with satisfaction, smiling at her.

"This is excellent coffee. Thanks." He sat back down, gently placing the cup on the short coffee table in front of the sofa.

Nancy sat at the end of the couch opposite him and again was very aware of how she must appear. She wiped the tea towel across her face again. Where was all this sweat coming from anyway! Oh yeah. Perimenopause. Sigh.

Doug again referred to his small notepad.

"The DA is pressing charges for DUI as an adult."

"Mom, that means the District Attorney is taking the guy to court as an adult for driving under the influence." Kate translated.

"Honey, I know what it means. Remember? I worked part time for an attorney before I had you."

Nancy remembered that time clearly. Her boss, Brad Harris had hired her knowing full well that she was planning on getting pregnant. He offered her the job, as well as the health insurance, and was reluctant to see her leave at seven months into the pregnancy. She organized his office for him, he covered her medical expenses. Jonathon was working freelance at the time and hadn't any insurance. Brad and his wife still kept in touch through Christmas cards every other year or so.

"Although you don't really have a say in the DA's filing, I wanted to let you know about it." Doug was leaning forward and looking around at everyone.

"How old was the guy?" Christy asked.

"Seventeen. He'll be eighteen tomorrow."

"What happened?" Nancy felt sorry for the kid even though he'd caused the accident.

"He was drunk and didn't see the light. His parents have all but disowned him. They're embarrassed at his behavior." Doug watched to see Nancy's reaction.

"Oh, that poor kid. Where is he now?"

"Out on bail, pending trial. He's living with his aunt."

"Does he understand the consequences?"

"He's not talking much. I don't think he's being callous, just quiet."

Doug put away his notebook, stood up and adjusted his heavy belt. It looked like it weighed at least 25 pounds. "Anyway, I just wanted to let you know what was happening. The DA will expect your kids to testify against the boy."

Nancy looked at her girls who were looking back at her.

"Isn't this going to ruin his life, if he's prosecuted as an adult?" Kate was always able to cut to the chase.

"Probably. It all depends on how hard the DA presses." Doug made eye contact with all four of the kids.

"Is there anything we can do?" Christy was the one who took in every stray dog, cat, or fellow student needing help. Nancy found a different young person sitting at her Sunday dinner table almost every week.

"I think he deserves everything he gets!" Joey was hard-nosed about a lot of things, and this appeared to be another one. Kate pushed his shoulder.

"Joey! Have some compassion. He's younger than you! And it sure doesn't sound as if his parents care at all."

Joey shoved his hands back into his pockets and looked sullen.

Nancy figured that Kate would end the relationship this weekend if not sooner. Kate didn't tolerate inhumanity very well.

"Thank you for coming by. I know that you're probably really busy and all." Nancy stood and waited for the officer to head for the front door.

Doug grabbed the coffee cup, tilted his head back and drained it. Nancy hadn't noticed a man's throat in a while. Officer Saunders had a very nice throat, and neck, and shoulders...

Nancy started when Doug spoke again.

"Thank you for the coffee, Ms. Adams." He handed her the empty cup.

Nancy smiled at the fact that he'd emphasized the 'Ms.'

As Doug walked out through the front door, he turned back to Nancy who had her hand on the doorknob.

"You ARE good in the kitchen." With that he winked, put on his sunglasses, smiled and walked out to the police unit parked at the end of Nancy's driveway. She could hear him say something into his lapel mike and the static reply.

Nancy stood there watching him until the black and white unit pulled into the street. As he drove away, Doug waved.

Nancy smiled and waved back.

"Nice view!"

Nancy turned to see both Kate and Christy crowded behind her, grinning at her.

She shut the door, opened her mouth a couple of times, couldn't think of anything to say, turned and walked into the kitchen to clean up. Behind her she could hear the girls giggling.

"He's cute! Old -- but cute." Kate followed Nancy into the kitchen and pulled a bowl out of the cupboard and filled it with cereal and milk.

"Better than that! He thinks Mom's cute, too!" Christy chimed in while she joined Kate at the dining table for cereal.

"Who thinks Mom's cute?" Jackson entered and took the chair next to Christy helping himself to the cereal and milk. Christy got up and got another bowl and spoon for herself while smiling at Jackson.

"I'm hungry, too." Joey exclaimed after following Jackson into the kitchen.

Kate appeared to be very busy with her cereal and Joey had to fend for himself. Christy took pity on him and handed him a bowl and spoon.

Nancy found it disconcerting to be spoken of as though she wasn't present, but she continued to do the dishes. She found herself smiling while she thought of the way Doug had winked at her. It had been a VERY long time since a male had winked at her! In fact, she couldn't recall Jonathan ever winking at her. Yet here was a really good-looking guy winking and grinning at her. It made HER grin just thinking about it.

Nancy didn't notice her kids nudge each other when she left the kitchen and went down the hall to her bedroom.

So this is what floating on a cloud feels like!

Nancy went into her bathroom and looked in the mirror.

Big mistake. Officer Saunders hadn't been smiling at her; he'd been trying not to laugh out loud!

Her hair was flying all over. She didn't have on any make-up, so every wrinkle and pore seemed to stand out. And the only thing she could say about the shirt was that the faded navy at least went nicely with her coloring.

Nancy sighed to herself and while disrobing and hopping into the shower, made a mental list of what she intended to do about her hair (highlights?), her hands (manicure?) and her face (plastic surgery?) Just kidding.

However, for the first time in an awful long time, Nancy was concerned about her appearance and wanted to look attractive.

In fact, it had been so long that she almost didn't recognize the feeling.

As she lathered up her hair she started humming an old Shirelle's love song. Wait… could have been the Chiffons.

CHAPTER 7

Doug shut his locker, secured the lock and turned to stare hard at Bill, who had also just closed his locker. Doug adjusted his belt and checked to ensure he had everything in its place.

Bill Winston was performing a mirror-image of what Doug was doing. It was 6:00 in the morning on Halloween and their 12 hour shift at the Orange Police Department was about to begin.

With eyes still locked, they both scooped up their caps at the same time and went down the hall to the briefing room. Doug's mouth was hardened into a straight line. Bill was smirking.

Grabbing a cup of coffee on the way in, Doug settled behind a desk towards the front of the room and scooted over very reluctantly when Bill joined him at the small table, crowding him to one side.

"So. Have you made up your mind yet?"

Doug took a sip of his coffee and didn't answer.

"Come on, Doug. It won't kill you."

Doug took a larger sip of his coffee.

"I'll bet you're just chicken."

Doug took a good sized drink, finished the cup and set it down a little harder than usual.

"What's the worst that could happen, huh?"

Doug gave Bill a sideways glance that would have made other men back down.

But Bill wasn't other men. He had known and worked with Doug for better than twenty years and considered himself to be Doug's best friend. Bill and his wife, Patty, had watched Doug date over the years, and had tried several times to fix Doug up with someone. They wanted Doug to be as happy as they were.

Doug had insisted that he was satisfied to be single and loved his job too much to even think about marrying and putting a wife through the hard task of being a cop's wife.

Patty had tried explaining to Doug that not all women considered it a burden; that many thought of their husbands as everyday heroes and it made their marriages special because they understood the difficulties their husbands had to deal with on a day to day basis.

Doug would just shrug and change the subject.

Now Doug had made the mistake of letting Bill know that he was interested in someone. And not just any someone. But someone who was so different from all the other women he'd dated that Bill's radar went on high alert. When Bill's radar went on high alert so did Patty's. And now Doug had to deal with questions.

Well, Doug grimaced, *better Bill than Patty*. When that woman got her teeth into something, she was worse than a wolf hound and wouldn't let go. Maybe Bill would back off if Doug gave him some information.

"Her name's Nancy."

"And?"

"And what?" Doug scowled again.

"And so are you going to ask her out?"

"We've only spoken a couple of times. I'm not sure she's even interested in me." This last was muttered under his breath, but Bill had ears like sonar.

"Come on, buddy. What woman wouldn't be interested in you? You're witty, charming and a barrel of laughs." Bill's sarcasm could have further irritated Doug, except he knew that underneath it was a true, caring friend.

Doug sat still for a moment and realized that Bill was right. What was the worst that could happen? She'd say no, and he was right back where he'd started.

Except something was different about Ms. Nancy Adams, and he felt he'd rather live with a 'what-if' hopefulness than a for certain 'no' from her.

Yeah, she sure was different. Usually he went for the Orange County highlighted blond hair, acrylic nails, and toned body from working out at a gym 4 days a week. He'd date the gal for a couple of weeks and then they'd go their separate ways, usually when the woman became aware that Doug wasn't interested in a long term relationship. Bill liked to tease Doug that he was getting his dates from a cookie-cutter assembly line of Barbie wannabes. The only saving grace was that the women were also smart. Doug did not suffer fools easily. He saw on a daily basis what happened when not so bright people had dealings with other not so bright people. It was a shame too, because the last woman he'd dated had absolutely nothing wrong with her. Doug just didn't feel anything stronger than physical attraction.

And now his attention was so stuck on Nancy, he'd turned down two come-on's he'd received while on the job over the past 3 weeks.

He wasn't sure if it was the way she really loved her kids, or the way she got so easily flustered every time he looked at her. It was cute. Also, she wasn't pretentious. It was refreshing. However, none of that explained how strongly he was drawn to her. He'd never felt this way about any other woman, and he sure couldn't explain it, even to himself. When he saw Bill staring at him, he relented.

"Adams."

"What?" Bill leaned in exaggeratedly with one hand cupped around his ear.

"Her last name is Adams." Doug swallowed a sigh of relief when the sergeant stepped to the front of the room and started the briefing.

"Okay, listen up. Remember, gang. Today is Halloween and we should expect all the usual shenanigans that go along with it." Sgt. Peters was no more Irish than Doug was, but because he'd been born on St. Patrick's Day, he'd adopted the green isle as his native homeland and everyone was used to him throwing out words he considered sounded Irish.

"Saunders, Winston, you'll be having the school duty. Make sure ta stop by the different carnivals throughout the late afternoon. There are a couple of candy bags for ya at the back table. Be sure and pass out the candy and pencils to the kids at the schools. It's part of the Chief's new PR program for the department."

Doug and Bill smiled and waved good-naturedly as they received hoots, hollers and wisecracks from the other officers in the room about pulling vacation duty.

The rest of the briefing was short and Doug and Bill were on their way to their units in no time with sacks of candy and boxes of pencils tucked under their arms.

After tossing the loot into the front passenger seat, Bill rested his arms across the door of his black and white and looked over at Doug.

"Well? Are you gonna ask her out?"

Doug debated for a couple of seconds and decided it would be easier to do that than suffer through several more days of nagging from Bill.

"Yes, I'll ask her out. There, are you happy?"

"Not yet. Bring her by the house and let Patty have a look at her."

"Huh-uh. No way, Bill. The both of you would scare her off for sure, what with all your questions and suggestions. You'll meet her when I'm ready for you to meet her."

Doug slid behind the wheel of his own unit and checked to ensure that everything was in order. As usual, the unit's computer was running in top condition. Sparky, the man in charge of the department's computers and electronic devices took extreme pride in the fact that his department's equipment was hardly ever on the fritz. The officers were thankful, too. The last guy in charge of the computers had been sincere, but not very fast when it came to repairs. Thank gawd he'd retired and they'd hired a kid straight out of college. Sparky was a computer nerd in the very best sense of the word. Equipment that would not work for anyone else, purred at top speed and efficiency for Sparky. Also the fact that he could produce a top-of-the-line flash-bang, made him even more popular with the SWAT team guys. What was it about things that went "boom" that made guys happy? Any age guys.

Doug pulled out of the parking lot after Bill did, and turned right onto Main Street from Struck. At Katella he turned right again and headed out for Cambridge Elementary as his first stop of the afternoon.

Doug enjoyed working for the City of Orange. He'd been on the force for the past twenty-six years and knew every section of the city, as well as a good portion of its populace. Several years earlier he'd been promoted, but found that he wasn't suited for sitting behind a desk. He did his best work dealing daily with the citizens and business owners of the city. After giving the desk job a year, he requested to be put back on a beat, and no one gave him a hard time for it. He knew it wasn't the best career move, but he'd rather be happy with his work and settle for a few less dollars, than continue to be frustrated with the politics of the profession.

His favorite part of the job was when he helped put together the bicycle safety classes for the local schools.

Which reminded him of last week.

He'd been assigned to run the safety class at a local private school. Since it was such a small school, there'd only been himself and Mike, another officer he liked working with. Both he and Mike were good with kids and it made for a rewarding day for both of them. And for Doug, more than just civic duty.

When he'd headed into the principal's office to confirm where to set up the event, he ran into Nancy Adams as she came out of the office.

They'd stopped about two feet from each other, said "Hi" and then just stood there smiling at each other.

There was no embarrassment from either of them; that is, until the school secretary giggled.

Nancy was the first to speak. "It's good to see you again, Doug. What are you doing here?"

"Running the bicycle safety class. Will you be there?"

"I wish. No, I'm the Drama Teacher. The homeroom teachers will be the ones taking the students to your class. Where are you holding it?"

"I was just about to explain that all to him, Ms. Adams." The principal, Victoria Newman smiled to soften her words.

"And you probably need to get to class." Doug didn't want to see Nancy go, but he couldn't figure out any other way to make her stay, especially when he had to speak with the principal.

"I do. If you get the chance, stop by the theatre. We're in rehearsal for a skit that the younger students will be doing at our Halloween Carnival." Then she realized that Doug would be working with students all day, and probably wouldn't have the time to stop by.

"If I can, I will." When Doug saw Nancy's smile dim slightly, he added, "I'd really like to see you."

Nancy's smile widened again, and she almost tripped when she started walking because she wasn't paying attention to where she was going. *I can't believe I'm such a klutz around him! He's going to think I'm perpetually clumsy.* Nancy tried to maintain some form of dignity, but found it next to impossible to stop smiling at Doug. Who, in turn, couldn't stop smiled at her.

If it hadn't been for Mrs. Newman, they probably would have stood there all day, lost in smiling at each other.

Fortunately, Nancy was able to make it to her class on time.

Unfortunately, Nancy's advanced drama class let out late, and Doug got called away as soon as the bicycle safety class was finished.

They both felt an odd combination of feeling let down, yet exhilarated because they'd seen each other.

Later that afternoon, as Nancy unlocked her car to go home, she thought to herself, "Is this what a crush feels like at my age?"

Throughout the rest of that day, Doug found himself smiling for no reason.

PAT ADEFF

CHAPTER 8

Nancy grinned as she walked across campus to her classroom. She took in a deep breath and felt almost giddy.

Nancy loved everything about autumn. She loved the smell of the air. The crispness that heralded the coming of colder weather. She even enjoyed the Santa Ana winds that kicked up now and again. This time of year always made her feel good. Another thing that made her feel good lately was whenever she spied a black and white unit drive slowly past her house. She liked to think that it might be that nice Officer Saunders. Then she would squelch the thought as though it was something forbidden.

Nancy was really enjoying her class at the private school where she worked. Although she was first and foremost a drama teacher, they'd found she had a natural talent for making math understandable to students who were previously having trouble, so they'd also given her a couple of math classes a week. With only ten students in each class, it was more like tutoring than teaching.

She felt that she was making a big difference for these kids, watching them comprehend fractions and long division. The look on the students' faces when they finally understood the concept was worth all of the struggles and frustration getting there.

Also, the school was having her favorite fundraiser that evening; the annual Halloween Carnival! Two years ago the school had vacillated on whether to call it a Halloween Carnival or a Fall Festival, after one of the new moms became upset that they were "celebrating the devil."

Well, it turned out that the lady wasn't interested in having any sort of conversation about it, since she knew that she was right and the school was wrong. In the end, the woman removed her child (who had never been able to do anything up to her mother's standards anyway) and homeschooled her. Nancy felt sorry for the little girl. The girl liked to sing and had an excellent voice, but the mother felt that singing was against God. Even though it was difficult, sometimes you just had to let some of them go and hope their lives turned out okay. However, that didn't make it any less heartbreaking.

The rest of the families were just fine with a Halloween Carnival and enjoyed bobbing for apples, the bean-bag toss, fishing for prizes and pie eating contests that were part of the festivities.

One of the booths that raised a lot of money for the school was the Fortune Telling booth. Nancy as the Performing Arts teacher, and a couple of the older girls would deck out one of the outside lunch areas with a tent, put up a bunch of scarves, tassels, and old jewelry, light some incense and pretend to tell fortunes.

The fortunes ran along the lines of "Ah! I see that you need to work harder on your math homework!" or "I see that you have a boyfriend! Does his name begin with a 'G'?" The kids loved it and it was fun for everyone.

Nancy had fun with it, too, since she got a chance to perform (with a very bad accent, which ranged throughout the evening from Middle Croatia to Minnesota.) She wore an awful wig that looked as though someone had put the world's largest brillo pad on her head, and more clanky jewelry than any respectable fortune teller would ever wear. It was clichéd, but fun.

The carnival finally got underway and Nancy had been telling fortunes for about an hour. The draped door was pulled aside as Nancy's next customer entered.

"Come into my parlor," Nancy tried to make it sound mysterious.

"You have come to have me tell your future - yes?" Nancy looked up just then at the person standing in front of her.

And stopped.

Doug Saunders was there in all his uniformed glory. Shiny black lace-up shoes, pressed slacks, heavy utility belt, crisp uniform shirt over Nancy's favorite part, the Kevlar vest. When her eyes reached his, she realized that she'd been staring at him with her mouth hanging open.

Her mouth snapped shut in mortification. Nancy couldn't believe that only the third time he'd seen her, she was now in one of the most ridiculous costumes imaginable. She sighed inwardly. Well, at least it's different than her cleaning-house ensemble.

"Ah! A member of our protection forces. A modern knight in armor! Please sit down and allow Madame Futurenata to tell your fortune. Yea, mon?" Now the accent had moved to Jamaica.

Doug removed his cap and sunglasses and settled himself into the cushy draped chair across from the small round table in front of Nancy.

It didn't help that he was starting to smile as he took in all of Nancy's gloriously over-the-top attire.

"You look...ah...in character?" Doug's grin threatened to get even wider.

"Madame Futurenata sees all and tells all." Nancy was trying her best to pretend that she wasn't absolutely dying inside. "Are you here to see into your future?"

"Yes, please." Doug put his cap on the floor next to his chair, sat up and waited.

Nancy raised both her arms a few inches, shook the forty bracelets she was wearing, so that they clamored and reached out her hands toward Doug. "Give me your hand." Nancy always looked at the person's palm as though she could actually read it. This gave her time to make up a fortune, based on the facts she already knew about the person.

As she took Doug's hand and turned it over she felt her chest get tight. Then she started to blush! She couldn't believe that holding this man's hand would cause this sort of reaction in her. The sort of reaction she hadn't felt in years.

"I see much hard work in your life." Nancy's voice now sounded like she was from Louisiana, as she ran her fingers over the calluses on the palm of his hand.

He leaned in closer, like he was also looking into his palm to see what was there. Their heads were inches apart.

Nancy's first thought was thank goodness she was chewing peppermint gum. She didn't like to offend the students with "coffee-breath" so she always chewed mint gum. Coffee was one of her remaining bad habits. She'd given up smoking after trying it for two months after Jonathon and she had split up. She didn't drink much more than a glass of plum wine or a cold beer once in a blue moon. And she sure as heck hadn't had sex for several years now. She'd been able to bury that urge when she realized her girls needed her first and foremost. Okay, okay, so approaching menopause had helped too.

But right now she was holding the hand of one of nature's more excellent specimens of human male. She could smell him. It was a clean crisp smell, Dial soap and 100% male, blended with the subtle undertone of pressed cotton and gun oil. When he exhaled she could smell coffee on his breath. It was nice, not sour. He smelled healthy. And virile. And entirely too good.

"I also see a female..." Nancy let her voice trail off, waiting for him to fill in the blank. She thought she was being subtle.

He saw right through her ploy and just grinned. "Huh-uh. I'm not giving any hints. I want my money's worth! Fifty cents is a lot of money and I expect to find out my future."

Nancy smiled back and then realized that he was probably staring at her mouth because of the garish purply-red lipstick that was part of her character make-up. Her guess was that it was also on her teeth.

Even though she had to consciously make herself relax, she hoped she appeared to not react at all to his proximity, while she tried to surreptitiously run her tongue over her teeth.

"I see a female. A blond. The picture is vague and blurry. Please let me concentrate for a moment." Nancy was struggling to come up with something, anything to say. Usually this was just plain old fun, but now it seemed her mind had gone on vacation.

While inhaling all the pheromones that were swirling around and affecting her in oh, so many delicious ways, artistic inspiration struck.

"I see flashing red and blue lights. I see a small curly-haired blond, clinging to you. I see many people grateful to you. I see..." Nancy stopped as Doug pulled his hand back.

She looked up into his face and saw his expression.

"I'm sorry... I'm... What did I say? I was just making it up. Doug, I'm sorry... I'm..." Nancy was stumbling around trying to find the words that would put him back at ease.

He swiped his hand over his face, inhaled deeply, and exhaled in a whoosh. His smile was shaky, but the color was coming back.

"Sorry about that. I forgot for a minute it was pretend. You hit really close to something for me. Give me a minute." Doug's voice was getting back to normal.

Nancy instinctively reached out and took his hand back, but this time she held it between both of hers giving comfort.

"I'm sorry. I really didn't mean to cause that reaction for you. Do you want some water?" Nancy reached under the table and grabbed one of the bottles of water she kept there during the carnival.

"Yeah. I'd like that." He accepted the bottle, unscrewed the cap, put the bottle to his lips and drained it, similar to what he did with the coffee at her house.

Now seeming to be fully in control and back to normal, he wiped his mouth with the back of his hand, put the cap back on the bottle and looked around for a trash can.

Nancy reached out her hand for the bottle. "I don't keep a trash can in here. I'll just put it with the rest of the bottles under my table. Recycling."

Doug handed the bottle to Nancy, but held onto it when she tried to take it from him.

"Dinner." He looked straight into her eyes.

"What?" Nancy was so startled, she dropped the accent.

"Dinner." He still held onto the bottle.

"Okay." What was she thinking?

Now it was his turn to pause. "Okay?"

"Yeah. Okay." Nancy gave a small smile. "When?"

"Tonight?" He was starting to smile, too.

"No. Not looking like this." Nancy waved her free hand towards her wig and outfit.

"Just change out of your costume, or whatever you call it. We can go after I get off my shift."

"No. You don't understand. When this wig comes off, my hair is plastered to my head, this awful lipstick has stained my mouth, and I've been sweating in this 'gypsy tent' for five hours. You would NOT want to be around me then." Nancy was nothing if not honest.

Doug found her honesty charming. She sure wasn't trying to impress him. He found that intriguing and so unlike any of the other women he'd dated.

"When, then?" Releasing the bottle, he stood up and gathered his cap under his arm. The arm that was right next to his Kevlar-vested chest. Nancy shot her eyes up to his and blushed again when she realized Doug had caught her ogling.

"Uh. Tomorrow?" Her voice sounded somewhat breathless.

"Sorry, no." He just looked at her. Nancy bet those eyes could make any criminal confess on the spot.

Then Nancy's insecurity kicked in. "Oh. Okay. I'm not sure then. But, thank you anyway for the offer." Nancy put on her best pretend smile; the one she'd perfected getting through the divorce.

"Tonight. 9:00. That should give you plenty of time to go home and do whatever it is you do to get ready." He didn't sound high-handed, just sure.

"Oh! 9:00. Oh, well, I suppose that could work. I'll have to see if my aide and the older girls could help put all this away after the carnival." Nancy stood up and waited for him to precede her through the draped door. He just stood there smiling at her and her insane outfit. She finally took a deep breath and squeezed by him when it seemed he wasn't going to move an inch, and pulled the drapery door back to ask Tess for her help.

As Nancy opened her mouth to speak, Tess, Kate, Christy, Jackson and the two high school girl helpers each said some form of "Go already! We'll clean up."

Nancy realized that her behind-curtains encounter with Officer Saunders had a listening audience. She turned around, embarrassed beyond belief to see Doug's grin.

"Thanks, guys. I'll have her home before midnight." He was in cahoots with them! "Pick you up at 9:00. Nothing fancy." With that he settled his cap on his head and left.

Nancy watched Doug walk away. He stopped, leaned over and reached into a sack when three little Storm Troopers ran up to him for candy.

Nancy found herself watching the way the muscles in his thighs bunched when he hunkered down in order to be at eye level with the kids. Her breath caught in her throat and she turned around rapidly to prevent anyone catching her checking out the cop!

Too late. Tess, her girls and the others were all grinning at her. Again at a loss for words, she just turned and went back into the fortune telling booth to get ready for her next customer. However, she couldn't seem to keep the smile off her face while she settled into her spot behind the small round table.

Her mind wandered several times as well as her accent, which continued to travel far and wide throughout the rest of the evening.

Doug found himself feeling young again. About the same way he had when Sally Sneed had agreed to go to the Spring Fling dance with him in 10th grade. He called his buddy Mike to cover for him, and was able to get off his shift a few minutes earlier than usual.

He made it to his house and pulled into the drive. Turning off the engine he looked at the front of the house – and smiled. He'd purchased the house on Cambridge Avenue fifteen years ago when it was in dire need of repair. He'd gotten it for an excellent price, and with the housing market moving at a steady climb over the past five years, he'd refinanced it and used the money to fix it up. Luckily he'd paid it all back before the market took another nosedive.

The front of the house now had a low river rock wall that Doug had constructed himself. He remembered days and days of hauling rocks to his house from the Santa Ana River bed. The low wall contained a four foot wide and eighteen foot long succulent garden, as well as several Jack-o-lanterns on the wall itself.

The front lawn was kept in very good shape by Doug's own hands, as were the well-maintained bushes that lined the front of the yard and ran up the side of the house to the back yard.

The driveway was cobblestoned with smaller river rocks that matched the low wall and gave a cottage feel to the house.

The house itself was painted a warm white with the windows and trim done in a cobalt blue that made the whole house look very clean and masculine. It had sure taken the paint salesman at the hardware store quite a while to convince Doug. But once the house was done, Doug was very pleased with the result.

As much as the outside was perfect for the City of Orange's Historical District where Doug lived, the best was inside.

When he'd first bought the place, it had dark wood floors and avocado green walls. It had been hideous. Doug stripped the floors back to their warm wood tone and painted the walls a natural cream color. Doug tore out the cottage cheese ceiling in the living room and had found an old pressed-tin ceiling two feet higher. It was in excellent condition and easy to renovate.

He then river-rocked the front of the fireplace and replaced the mantle with a 12"x5' unfinished piece of teak that matched the floors completely. He's spent weeks honing that piece of wood to the satin sheen that it now was.

In the master bathroom he tore out the 1950's upgrade from the previous owner, and installed more river rock in the shower. It looked like an outdoor waterfall took up one complete side of the bathroom.

Although the rest of the house was country-warm, the kitchen was all modern. Black and sleek chrome. He even had a Viking refrigerator built in along one wall. The breakfast area that led out to the backyard was where Doug ate most of his meals.

As he changed out of his clothes, Doug turned on the taps in the shower. He then looked at himself in the mirror, turning to the side the way all guys do, and flexed his arms and his "six pack" stomach. He was pleased to see that all the time he spent keeping himself in shape for the job, kept him from looking like most other guys his age.

Yeah, he had more wrinkles around his eyes and mouth, and more gray in his hair, but he thought he still looked OK.

The water was steaming out of the shower, so Doug stepped in and started shampooing his hair. Washing off the sweat of the day, he entertained a little fantasy about how Nancy would look in his shower – all wet and slippery and woman.

He reached over and turned the cold spigot all the way on and the hot spigot all the way off. He was amazed at how rapidly he'd responded to the thought of making love to the woman.

Time for a cold shower!

CHAPTER 9

Whatever had she been thinking!

Nancy was frantically towel-drying her hair and desperately wishing that she had never agreed to dinner. She glanced at the clock and realized that Doug would be here any minute!

She hadn't meant to stay as late as she had at the carnival. It was just that so many of the children wanted their fortunes told, and she hated to disappoint the kids. So she'd kept the fortune telling booth open even after the carnival had officially closed for the evening. She didn't escape until Victoria, the principal, had come over and shooed all the students back to their parents to go home.

That had been 8:00 pm and now it was 8:55 and her hair wasn't dry, she didn't have on any make-up yet, and for sure hadn't decided what to wear.

Oh, no! Was that the doorbell?

Nancy heard Kate's voice from down the hall and through her closed bedroom door.

"Hi! Come on in! Mom should be ready in a minute. I'll tell her you're here."

Nancy heard Kate's footsteps come down the hall and the knock on her bedroom door.

"Come on in, Honey." Nancy called out and the door opened.

"Oh, Mom! You're not even close to ready!" Kate exclaimed while closing the door behind her.

"Kate, am I doing the right thing?" Nancy felt like there was a chorus line of butterflies doing high kicks in her stomach.

"If by doing the right thing, you mean having dinner with a law-abiding officer of our community who also happens to be a handsome member of the opposite sex, then yes." Sometimes Kate could put things in perspective very rapidly.

"Yeah, but what if he's..." Nancy had almost said the thing that had been on her mind since Doug had asked her to dinner. *What if he's younger than me?* She just couldn't bring herself to utter the words, even to Kate. Must be some of that early 'what's proper' training from her youth.

Kate dove into Nancy's closet and pulled out an outfit. When Nancy saw the black jeans and pumpkin-colored sweater, she started to protest.

"Honey! I can't wear that to dinner!"

"Okay. But if you wear anything fancier, you'll be way overdressed. He's wearing jeans and a sweatshirt. Besides, the sweater's color brings out your eyes."

"Oh." Nancy was somewhat taken aback. "Oh, okay. Good. Well then." She went into her bathroom and turned the hair dryer towards her hair, wishing that she'd spent money on highlights.

"Mom, do you want your boots or sneakers?" Kate's voice was muffled by the closet doors behind which her head was buried.

Nancy turned off the hair dryer and loudly whispered, "What's he wearing?"

"I'll go look." Kate loudly whispered back with an impish grin. Then she hurried out of the room before Nancy could stop her.

Oh, for Pete's sake! The man is going to think we're nuts.

Within seconds Kate was back and closed the door behind her.

"Boots. Definitely boots." Kate's smile was huge and contained a bit of the-cat-who-ate-the-canary to it.

Nancy finished blow-drying her hair and threw on some make-up. Oh how she wished the costume lipstick hadn't stained her mouth. Maybe if she put a light gloss over it, it would even out.

Finally, after pulling on her jeans (why hadn't she'd lost those 12 pounds?) and putting on her sweater (too bright? too tight?) she decided that she was as ready as she was going to get.

"You look fine, Mom! In fact, you look really good." Kate was handing Nancy her purse. "Do you have money? Your cell phone?"

Pausing, Nancy and Kate looked at each other and then burst out laughing. When had their roles reversed?

Nancy walked out into the living room. Doug stood up from the couch when she entered. His jeans fit just right and his sweatshirt proved that he sure kept himself in shape. He looked great!

"You look great!"

"Thank you," she managed to say. Deep breath - she was really nervous.

"You ready?" Along with the faded jeans and a police department sweatshirt, Doug had on cowboy boots, and his hair was sort of standing up. That's when Nancy noticed the pair of helmets on the coffee table.

"We're riding a motorcycle?"

Doug seemed to hesitate. "Yeah. Is that all right with you?"

"Oh, yes! I love motorcycles!" Nancy hadn't ridden in years. Jonathon used to own a touring bike, but it had become less and less fun to ride with him, and Nancy didn't ride on her own.

Doug's smile came back. "Good!" He walked forward, carrying the two helmets, one in each hand. "Let's go, then." Oh my! His walk was 90% male, 10% predator and 100% exciting! Nancy felt her pulse already starting to race.

To hide her embarrassment, she turned towards the door where she found Kate, Christy and Jackson lined up, grinning like the village idiots.

Nancy smiled and shook her head. "What's this?"

Jackson spoke first. "What time will you be home?"

"And where are you going?" chimed in Christy.

Doug became solemn and stepped forward. "We'll be at the Steak 'n Stuff on Lincoln Avenue, probably stay awhile for the band, and then I'll have her home before midnight since it's a school night. Okay with you?"

The three idiot-grinners just continued to smile and nod.

"Sure, that'll be fine. We'll wait up for her." Kate sounded pleased; and somehow grown up and in charge.

Nancy gave quick kisses to all of them and went out the door. "See you guys later. Love you."

"Love you, Mom." "Bye! Have fun!" The door closed behind Nancy and Doug as they walked over to the motorcycle.

"You have a wonderful family," Doug said as they approached the bike.

"They're my whole life," Nancy quietly answered. Then she spotted the motorcycle.

"It's a Honda Valkyrie!" Nancy loved motorcycles and her smile showed it.

Doug threw Nancy a lopsided grin. "You know what this is?"

"Yep, and I also know that it would win hands-down in a race against my car." Nancy was running her hand over the bike. "She's gorgeous!"

"Yeah, I'm real fond of her too. I worked for quite a while to get her just the way I wanted her. At first I wasn't sure about the color." Doug watched as Nancy's hand followed the contours of the bike. He swallowed as his imagination took flight.

"Cobalt blue is the best color ever!" Nancy almost added, *'In fact it matches your eyes,'* but didn't.

Doug reached over and put the helmet on Nancy's head. She reached into the sides of it and pushed her hair back.

"You realize that my hair is going to look awful when I take this helmet off, don't you?" Nancy felt she had to warn him.

"It really couldn't look any worse than that sorry excuse for a wig you were wearing today." Doug laughed and ducked as Nancy gave a small swat in the direction of his head.

Nancy couldn't believe herself. She was flirting! She couldn't remember the last time she'd done that. It sure as heck wasn't within the last two decades. Which brought her to the big question she'd been wanting to ask for a while now. How old WAS he? It was hard to guess his age. He looked to be different ages at different times. Right now, he looked to be about 10 years younger than her! Oh, that would be so embarrassing. What's that awful word everyone uses nowadays? Oh yeah – cougar.

He reached over and tightened the strap to her helmet. His fingers felt wonderful on her jawline and chin; which she almost forgot to hold up so that her throat would look thinner.

He patted the top of her helmet and threw his leg over the bike. He started it with ease, backed it around and indicated for her to hop on. She put her leg between Doug's back and the backrest she would be leaning on, and slid onto her seat. She'd almost forgotten what fun it was to ride!

The trip to the restaurant took about 15 minutes longer than it should, because Doug took a back way which was just beautiful. The air was soft and cool. The stars were bright, and the moon was three quarters full. The smell of orange blossoms was heady. There were a couple of late-night trick-or-treaters heading home and Doug rode carefully, conscious of the small people still out and about.

Nancy closed her eyes, inhaled deeply and sighed. Doug reached over and placed his hand on her knee which was next to him. It felt very right.

Nancy had forgotten that riding a motorcycle with someone was intimate, but in a different sort of way. Right now it just felt natural and good. Doug's driving made her feel very safe. He wasn't necessarily a slow driver, but he was very aware of the surrounding traffic and seemed to be able to foretell what the other drivers were going to do.

They arrived at the steak house and Doug carefully wended the motorcycle through a crowd of young adults standing in the parking lot, obviously under the influence. The guys were play-scuffling over something and the girls were giggling together, watching the mock-fight.

Doug parked the bike close to the front door. Nancy got off the bike, removed her helmet and ran her fingers through her hair, hoping against hope that it didn't look too bad.

Doug stood and removed his helmet, keeping his eyes on the young crowd. He unconsciously ran a hand through his hair to unflatten it. He had on what Nancy thought of as a *cop face*; intent and focused.

She noticed that Doug's attention was primarily on one young man in the group. She also noticed that Doug not only had on his *cop face*, but that in fact, his jaw was clenched pretty tight.

Handing her his helmet, Doug turned to Nancy. "Excuse me a moment. I'll be right back."

Nodding, Nancy moved closer to the motorcycle and watched him walk over to the group. She was too far away to hear anything, but saw Doug call out to the young man and wave him over.

The young man spotted Doug, looked away, and then crossed his muscled arms over his chest and refused to take a step. His jaw clenched in a manner very similar to Doug's.

Nancy watched as their conversation quickly became a heated argument. Although she could now hear their voices, she still could not make out what they were saying.

The other young people were standing off to one side and a couple of the girls were looking at the ground as though they were embarrassed by the conversation.

Finally Doug abruptly turned around and stalked back towards the motorcycle and Nancy. Beyond Doug, Nancy saw one of the other boys put a hand on the young man's shoulder, but he shook it off and strode in anger to a red Ford Mustang. One of the girls broke off from the rest of the crowd and ran to the car, jumping into the passenger seat right before the car shot out of the parking lot and into the street, its tires squealing.

When the car's tires screamed, Doug stopped walking and clenched his eyes shut, holding himself very still. He stayed that way for several moments. Finally he opened his eyes, saw Nancy and made himself relax.

Then as though the incident had not just happened, Doug smiled at Nancy and moved to her side. "Are you ready for some dinner?"

Nancy searched his eyes for some sign of upset, but could find none. She thought, *Okay, if that's the way this man handles his emotions, I'll follow his lead. If he wants to talk, he will.* She hadn't been overly disturbed by the event, and knew somehow that he would tell her about it when he was ready.

Doug was thankful Nancy didn't badger him with questions, or get hurt when he didn't want to talk, like some of the other women he'd dated. He smiled at her as he grabbed her hand and moved towards the restaurant door. Yes, she was someone very special.

Nancy loved the way it felt so natural for him to take her hand.

He opened the door and when he put his hand on the small of Nancy's back to escort her into the restaurant, both of their breaths caught. Oh, boy! This was gonna be some night.

Nancy was rapidly realizing how much she had missed affection from a man. And this particularly handsome man was dishing it out in spades!

....

Doug's a dad? He has a kid? A grown kid? What about an ex-wife?

Nancy wanted desperately to ask Doug questions, but knew intuitively that he needed to tell her in his own way.

They'd passed on drinks and appetizers and had ordered dinner directly since the kitchen was about to close.

Over salads and then steak dinners, Doug haltingly told Nancy about his son, the young man in the parking lot. Andy was in his mid 20's, but acted like he was still 17, staying out late, drinking too much and hanging with an irresponsible crowd.

Doug was somewhat surprised to find himself opening up to Nancy and telling her things that he'd never even told Bill and Patty. It just felt right to confide in her.

Andy's mom, Sue, and Doug had been rookies together on the force over 20 years ago. They had a brief stint as partners until one night after a really bad day at work where they'd had to fire their guns, wounding a robber, they'd gone to her apartment, had a few beers and one thing had led to another. They weren't in love, just in need of comfort. They were both surprised and chagrined when they woke up the next morning sharing a bed.

They didn't mention it again and managed to get assigned different shifts. Until a couple of months later when Sue met Doug in the parking lot and informed him that he was going to be a father.

Out of sheer shock and being young, he made the stupid mistake of asking if she was sure it was his. She wouldn't speak to him for another seven months.

Sue took maternity leave and he didn't hear from her until after the birth, when she handed him a copy of the birth certificate with his name on the line indicating "Father," and "Andrew Brandon" indicating his son's name.

Doug had asked her if she wanted him to give her any child support or to be a part of Andy's life in any way. At first she'd said "no," and Doug only saw them by chance once or twice a year. But later as Andy approached his teen years, Sue asked Doug to talk with him occasionally when Andy got into trouble.

However, by this time in his life, Andy had developed quite a bad case of "I hate Dad, because he never cared about me and abandoned us" and refused to listen to Doug's advice.

This frustrated Doug, because for years he'd wanted to help raise his son, but Andy's mother didn't want him in the picture and Doug felt he had to respect her wishes. Over time, watching Sue jump from one boyfriend to another, Doug found it easier to pretend he wasn't Andy's father, than to feel the frustration of watching the life she and Andy were living.

Lately Doug hadn't seen much of Andy, since the kid had been out of town trying to finish his bachelor's degree. The kid! See? Even Doug still thought of Andy as a kid.

Well, at least one of Nancy's questions had been answered. If Doug had fathered a son when he was around 25 years old, and that kid was now around 25 years himself, then Doug must be close to her age. Okay!

Which led to another question. Why was Doug still an officer with a beat? Why wasn't he in a suit or retired?

Nancy felt that on a first date, though, she couldn't really ask questions like that. First date! She still couldn't believe that she had accepted his invitation. She also couldn't believe that he'd asked her out while she'd been wearing that ridiculous outfit! The man was either blind or desperate, but he truly did not seem to be either!

By the time dinner was done and the band had started up in the bar area of the restaurant, the conversation had gotten back on more neutral ground, and Nancy and Doug were relaxed and enjoying each other's company, learning each other's facial expressions. They discovered that they were both avid Angel's Baseball fans, loved the beach at a stormy sunset, and both hated sushi. Finally a comfortable silence enveloped them, but only for a moment.

"Dance?" Doug nodded his head towards the dance floor.

Oh, boy! thought Nancy. This really IS a date!

"Love to!"

Doug paid the bill by leaving money on the tray as well as leaving a good tip for the waitress. Nancy was pleased to see that he wasn't a cheapskate like Jonathon. Wait! Where had that thought come from? She hadn't thought of Jonathon in weeks! Oh, well. Must be the fact that she was once again doing the man/woman thing. Oh, she was so out of practice.

However, the evening had been moving along with very few awkward moments, so far.

That is, right up until that moment when Doug pulled Nancy into his arms to dance. It had been so long since she'd been this close to a male that it took her several moments to relax. She felt like a skittish 14 year old at her first dance. Doug was a smooth dancer, and his hand felt nice and warm though the back of her sweater. Nancy finally relaxed in his arms and he pulled her closer.

Doug could smell the subtle scent of spring rain along with soap. God this woman smelled good and felt great in his arms. She was soft and feminine and fit just right. And her curves were making his mouth go dry.

Just as the Tobey Keith song was winding down to its finish, Nancy felt what she thought might be a soft kiss at her hairline. She pulled her head back to look up into Doug's face, but Doug pulled her in closer for a final quick spin as the song ended, and they ended up almost tripping over each other's feet. They laughed their way to a table closer to the dance floor and Doug caught the cocktail waitress' eye. He held up two fingers and she nodded and headed to the bar.

A few minutes later the waitress, dressed in her Halloween costume of Pirate Maiden, brought over two non-alcoholic beers, placed napkins on the table, and then the bottles on top of the napkins.

"Thanks, Roxie. On my tab?" Doug smiled at the waitress.

"Sure, Doug." Roxie smiled at him and moved to the next table, clearing off a couple of empty glasses and wiping down the water rings with a practiced sweep of her bar rag.

"I hope you don't mind that the beer is non-alcoholic. I just prefer not to drink." Doug sounded slightly embarrassed.

"Oh, no." Nancy replied. "I can either take it or leave it. I've never been much of a drinker myself."

Doug held up his bottle and Nancy raised hers and they clinked together in a toast.

"To a great evening with a fun date." Doug smiled and once again looked like he was in his 30's.

"Okay. I just have to ask. How old are you?" Nancy stammered her way through the question, then felt the heat rise up her chest and neck.

"I'm one year older than you." Doug looked at her unflinchingly and waited for Nancy's reply.

"Oh. Well. That's good!" Nancy took another swig of her beer and relaxed. Then another thought crossed her mind.

"How do you know how old I am?" Nancy was puzzled.

It was Doug's turn to stall for time now.

"I, uh. I found out."

"How?"

"I, um. I looked up your DMV record."

Nancy didn't know whether to be upset or flattered. She chose the latter.

"When did you do that?"

"The afternoon after I came to your house the first time."

Nancy and Doug looked into each other's eyes and something shifted between them. He reached out and took one of her hands in his. He ran his thumb over her palm and she became instantly aware of the calluses on her hand. Nancy tried to pull her hand back, but Doug hung onto it.

Nancy was trying to find a way to explain about how her hands were so rough because of the stagecrafts class she taught, when Doug said "I like your hands. They're honest hands."

Then he did something that caused Nancy's breath to catch in her throat. He raised her hand to his mouth and kissed her palm. She really hoped that her hand smelled clean after the motorcycle ride and dinner.

He kept her hand in his and smiled at her. Just then the band started up with a slow number and Doug pulled her to her feet, out onto the dance floor and into his arms.

The music was slow and they swayed in time, fitting closer and closer. Finally the music stopped and so did Doug and Nancy. They stood there for a heartbeat then pulled slightly apart.

Doug looked down into Nancy's face. He loved her face. Her skin was soft. Her eyes were honest and warm. Her lips were... her lips were stained purply-red... sort of.

Doug smiled into Nancy's eyes and asked "How did your husband ever let you go?"

Nancy's breath hitched and she pulled away from Doug. She really hadn't wanted to get into this on their first date. She wanted the magic to last a little longer.

Doug saw the haunted look that passed across Nancy's face and wished that he could take the words back.

"Nancy. I'm sorry. I didn't mean to upset you." He slid his hand down her arm and took her hand in his and led her back to their table. He held out her chair and waited for her to sit. As he leaned in to help push her chair in, Doug's senses were once again filled with just how right she smelled. Soap and spring rain.

He moved around to the other side of the table and sat down facing her. He took Nancy's hand in his again.

"I don't want to pressure you, but I would really like to know what happened with your marriage."

Nancy realized that Doug had opened up to her when he told her about his son; and now it was her turn to reciprocate.

She hadn't truly spoken to anyone about it before. But something told her that Doug wouldn't condemn her for anything she told him. She also knew somehow that she trusted him, completely. She felt safe.

So she explained how she'd met Jonathon. She told about their wedding, about when the girls were born, and how he'd asked her for a divorce several times throughout their marriage, but she'd always convinced him to work with her to hold the marriage together. The truth was, at the time, she knew she was the only one creating their marriage.

Nancy spoke of her humiliation at their last disastrous anniversary dinner, as well as later when she finally gave up and said yes, Jonathon could have his divorce.

Doug had sat quietly throughout Nancy's story, just holding her hand and noticing how much she seemed to blame herself. From where he sat, Jonathon was a class-A jerk.

Nancy was quietly looking at Doug's hand surrounding hers. Then she watched as he gathered both her hands in his.

Doug then looked into her eyes and said the perfect words.

"He was a fool to let you go."

Nancy's breath caught and held before she shakily replied, "Well, I've always thought so."

With that, both of them smiled and laughed.

Just then the band came back from their break and started up with a raucous song that had Doug and Nancy heading for the dance floor to join the crowd in their line dance.

Nancy loved the way that she always found Doug right next to her, or she'd bump into him and he'd "have to" put his arm around her or his hand on her waist.

Doug loved it even more than Nancy and that was saying something!

Neither of them could remember ever having had a more fun evening EVER in their lives. All too soon, it was time to go home.

The motorcycle ride was heavenly.

CHAPTER 10

The next day, Nancy went through the motions of teaching, but found herself frequently staring off into space, which would normally have caused her students to wonder, except that they were all still in sugar comas from the previous evening's Halloween festivities. Things worked out well that day in class. For once, teacher and pupils were on the same level.

She finally quit trying to teach anything new, and put on one of the movies in the Red Curtain Trilogy by Baz Luhrman. At least it was Shakespeare.

While her students got into the story of unrequited love between two people their own ages, Nancy was thinking the rest of her date had gone very nicely. And when Doug had walked her to her door at 11:55 pm, he'd taken both her hands in his, thanked her for a wonderful evening and then kissed her on the corner of her mouth.

And let me tell you! That soft kiss was more erotic than any full-on, open mouthed kiss that Nancy had EVER had! She'd tingled all the way from the top of her head to the tips of her toes. And a few places in between.

And every time she replayed that kiss, she felt the same sparks shoot through her again. *Oh! Good grief, Nancy! Get a grip.* It was an innocent kiss. *Yeah? Then why did it make her blood sing?* Maybe because it had been years since a man showed any interest? *Yeah. That must be it.* ANY kiss from any guy would have caused this reaction.

Liar.

There was something about Doug that was so different. She couldn't understand why some woman hadn't scooped him up yet.

"Ms. Adams? Excuse me, Ms. Adams?"

Nancy brought her attention back to the classroom and realized that the DVD was skipping and her students wanted her to fix it.

"Ms. Adams? Are you all right?"

"You bet, Diandra. Just suffering from a little sugar shock myself."

Eventually the bell rang and Nancy exhaled and relaxed while the students filed out for the weekend, calling good-bye to her. She straightened her desk and then sharpened all the pencils that she kept in a coffee can decorated like a panda bear on her desk. It had been one of the numerous crafts gifts that one of her students had given her over the years. And she'd kept every one of those gifts. She was finally erasing the chalkboard when she heard someone's throat clear behind her.

Doug had walked into her classroom after the students had left, only to find Nancy stretched up onto tiptoes, erasing the board. He found his throat close when her curvy backside moved from side to side in time with the eraser moving across the chalkboard. He cleared his throat and was about to say her name when Nancy swung around and found him standing just across the desk from her.

They were both holding their breaths and then slowly smiled at each other while silently exhaling.

Nancy was the first to find her voice. "Hi!"

"Hi, yourself." *Brilliant Doug. Say something else.*

"So, how did you survive the day after Halloween?" *Well it wasn't witty, but it would do.*

"It was the usual. You'd think someone would come up with a way to have Halloween on Fridays every year. It would sure make life easier." *Good! You sound almost normal, Nancy.*

"Look. I know there's some unwritten rule somewhere that I'm supposed to wait at least three days before calling you after a date, but I was in the neighborhood ... well actually I wasn't, truth be told. I decided to stop by and see if you'd like to go out again tonight." Doug wasn't sure if he'd made any sense, but he hoped Nancy had understood him.

When she didn't answer right away, Doug realized that he'd just assumed that she wasn't doing anything else. Wow, that was stupid! For all he knew, she had dates lined up for months to come. *Pretty arrogant, Saunders!*

"I'm sorry. I know this is short notice, and I'm sure you probably already have plans. Would you rather make it next week?"

"No."

No? As in 'No, I don't want to go out with you next week?' or 'No, I don't want to go out with you at all, ever again?' Doug looked down at his hat that he was turning around in his hands. He felt foolish. Unwise for coming by the day after their first date. Daft for just assuming she'd want to go out with him again. Brainless for standing in front of her desk like some recalcitrant 6th grader talking to their teacher.

"Tonight."

Tonight? He glanced back up into her face.

"Doug, I know I'm supposed to play coy and hold back and make you wait another week for our next date, but I just don't want to. I had a really great time last night, and I'd love to go out with you tonight." Nancy had decided that playing by The Rules wasn't going to work in this case. For all she knew, he'd be injured in the line of duty, and she'd spend the rest of her life wishing she'd grabbed the bull by the horns -- speaking metaphorically, of course.

Doug's smile said it all. "Great! I'll pick you up at 8:30 after I get off my shift. Would you like to catch a movie?"

"Yes." Nancy's smile answered his.

"All right. You pick out the movie. Is it okay with you if we take my bike again?"

"I wouldn't have it any other way." Nancy felt revved. Another date! Yes! And this time she wouldn't have to get up at 6:00 am the next morning in order to get ready for work!

Doug took a couple of halting steps towards Nancy and she shyly reciprocated. They met at the side of her desk and he leaned down to give her another soft kiss on the side of her mouth. She was really starting to like his kisses. When he pulled back and smiled into her eyes, all she could do was grin back at him.

He settled his cap on his head, pulled his sunglasses out of his pocket and grinning from ear to ear, put them on. He gave Nancy a little salute and walked out of her classroom.

Nancy stared as he exited, thinking, *Wow! How did someone like THAT want to date someone like her?*

If she'd known that what Doug had thought about all day was a lot more than just a date, she would have blushed from head to toe. Too late. She was already blushing. Wait. Hang on. It was another hot flash.

Nancy groaned and grabbed for the tissue box. As she swabbed her forehead, she had the thought that maybe she was just too old for this sort of thing.

Shaking her head ruefully, she decided, maybe so, but she was sure going to have fun while it lasted. It had been quite a while since a male -- a REAL male -- had made any moves on her at all.

Mr. Parks, the short, overweight science teacher didn't count. 'Come see my new Bunsen burner,' my eye!

Nancy hummed while she finished straightening up her desk, before she locked up and left for the day.

She hoped Kate was home and could help her find another outfit.

PAT ADEFF

CHAPTER 11

Actually Kate was thinking about the fact that she didn't have a date and it was Friday night. Oh, she'd been asked out, but she just didn't want to go out with Joey again. And Brett had turned out to be a flake.

Now that she was in college, she realized the type of person she really wanted to go out with was that cute doctor from the emergency room. He was smart, funny, competent and above all, responsible. But, short of having an emergency, she just didn't see any way of ever seeing him again. And she didn't think that pretending to have some emergency was the way to go about getting his attention.

She knew that Dr. Derek Coburn was single because she'd asked her friend Hilary who worked at the hospital in admitting.

"Kate, all the gals working here are after him." Hilary's news wasn't particularly upbeat.

"Okay. But is he serious about anyone?" Kate had decided that she was tired of sitting back and having some guy find her. She'd made the decision that she needed to go after what she wanted.

Unfortunately, she wasn't sure how to go about it.

"He hasn't seriously dated since he started working here last March. At least not that anyone here knows about."

"Hilary, do you know his schedule?" Kate held her breath, hoping against hope that Hilary wasn't going to laugh at her.

"No. But I can find out easily. I'll call you back." With that, Hilary hung up.

Hm-m-m. Kate figured that it wouldn't hurt if she happened to be freshly showered and nicely dressed with her hair and make-up done. Just in case.

Kate must have spent at least an hour getting ready, frequently checking her cell phone just in case Hilary had called and she hadn't heard the ring.

Just as she was about to give up, her phone rang.

"Kate? Hi, it's me. He's on ER duty tonight from 7:00 pm to 3:00 am. Good luck!"

Kate didn't even have time to thank her before the phone line went dead.

Okay, now she had the where and the when. She just needed to come up with a why.

She was walking down the hallway when she passed her mom's open bedroom door and couldn't help stopping and staring.

"Mom? What are you doing?!?"

Kate couldn't believe her eyes. Nancy's normally neat, precise bedroom looked like her closet had exploded all over everything! There were slacks draped all over the bed, blouses and sweaters hung from every available chair and dresser, and -- was that a pair of PANTYHOSE hanging from the ceiling fan?

"Mom? Where are you?"

"In here," Nancy replied in a quivering voice. Just then, she came out of her bathroom with a portable curling iron in one hand, smeared nail polish on her thumbnail and red eyes from crying.

"MOM?" What happened?" Kate moved towards her mom, in time for Nancy to fall into her arms crying. Kate grabbed the hot curling iron and held it away from them while Nancy sobbed on her shoulder.

"Oh, Kate! I don't know what to do! I'm not sure what to wear so I don't look fat. My hair is too plain, so I'm trying to fix it, but I'm just making a mess. And I can't seem to settle on a nail polish color!!! I've only got an hour and I haven't even chosen a movie yet!"

Kate held her mom at arm's length and looked her in the eye. "Mom. Pull it together. I am assuming that you have another date tonight. Right?"

At Nancy's nod, Kate smiled. There wasn't any catastrophe! Mom was just out of practice.

"Great! I'm also assuming it's with a certain member of our city's illustrious protection force?"

Nancy smiled and wiping her eyes nodded yes again.

Gently Kate said, "Okay. Good. First let's hang some of this stuff back up so we can find a nice outfit for you."

At that, Nancy looked around her room for the first real time since she'd dashed home and started going through her closet. Oh, my! How had all this happened? Nancy closed her eyes, sighed, opened them and looked at Kate. "I am seriously in trouble, you know that?"

Kate nodded and smiled. "Officer Saunders sure seems to be able to fluster you pretty good!"

Nancy looked embarrassed and started to pick up a sweater, but smeared her nail polish even more. "Oh, sugar!" Sighing and sitting on top of several pieces of clothing which had been haphazardly thrown on the bed, Nancy looked beseechingly at Kate. "Help?"

Kate set the curling iron on the shelf in the bathroom, grabbed a pair of slacks and started hanging things up. "I'd be more than happy to help! It's about time you started doing something nice for yourself."

"I do things for myself!" Nancy protested. "I do all sorts of things for myself!"

"Name one."

"Well, I -- I." Nancy paused while she tried to think of something. "I go to the library and check out my favorite authors!" *There! That was something.*

"Uh-huh. AFTER you've picked out plays and DVDs for your class. I mean something that is totally, one hundred percent just for you." Kate continued to hang up clothes while awaiting Nancy's reply.

"Okay. I get the point. It's been a while."

Kate grinned. "Yeah, but you sure make up for lost time!" She raised her eyebrows Groucho Marx style and gave a low whistle.

"Kate!" Nancy giggled, slightly horrified that she was listening to her daughter use that tone while discussing a male. Yet, she had to agree. Doug Saunders was definitely wiggling eyebrows, whistle material!

With Kate's help, it only took ten minutes to settle on an outfit for that evening. After Nancy had answered Kate's question about the mode of transportation, Kate pulled together stretch jeans, and a 3/4 sleeve olive-colored pullover sweater that brought out the green in Nancy's eyes.

Nancy removed her nail polish and Kate applied a single coat of "Angel Hair" gossamer pink. Then Kate made Nancy sit on the closed toilet seat while she repaired her hair.

"You know you're going to have helmet-head anyway, right?"

Nancy sighed. She wished she had the kind of thick hair that always sprang back into place. Like Doug's. His hair was perfect. It was dark with a smattering of gray at the temples, right next to his cobalt blue eyes.

Why is it that men seemed to get better with age? Gray hair and lines on their faces only added to their virility. While women just seemed to get stretch marks, crepey skin and a droopy chin? It just didn't seem fair. Yet, Nancy was not about to start going the plastic surgery/liposuction route. One of the teachers at the school had a face lift done last July and was still walking around looking surprised all the time. Nancy thought the doctor had gotten a little carried away around the forehead.

The thought of liposuction brought to mind the last time Jonathon had taken her out for dinner while they were still married...

PAT ADEFF

CHAPTER 12

Nancy couldn't believe it was their 20th wedding anniversary! Twenty years. Where had the time gone?

Last week, Jonathon had Nancy call and make reservations for them at a swanky restaurant in Laguna Niguel for tonight. Nancy had even had her hair and nails done that afternoon. She knew how much Jonathon liked it when she paid attention to her hair and make-up.

Nancy had found an outfit that showed off her green eyes. The girls had arranged sleep-overs at their friends' houses, so Nancy had all afternoon to get ready by herself. It had been so long since Jonathon had taken her out! She hoped the evening went well. He had been sort of distant recently, and Nancy was looking forward to putting their marriage back in good standing. Well, at least better.

She even applied Jonathon's favorite perfume to the back of her neck and the inside of her thighs. Wishful thinking. Jonathon hadn't paid much attention to her recently, and had NEVER kissed her on the back of the neck; even after she'd told him that it was an extremely sensitive, erotic spot for her. Maybe he just forgot. Yes, that must have been it. Because he also forgot that she'd told him that since she'd had the girls, it bothered her to have her abdomen touched, and yet that was always the first place his hand went when he wanted sex. Nancy didn't think she'd understand Jonathon in a million years. Although she really wanted to.

She was just slipping into her heels when she heard the back door open. Jonathon was home.

She came down the stairs and went into the kitchen where he was going through the mail.

"Hi, Hon!" She walked over to him, but he didn't look up from the stack of envelopes in his hand. Nancy leaned down and playfully looked up at him from over the envelopes.

Jonathon frowned slightly and moved his hand to the side, so that he could finish reading the return address label on one of the envelopes.

Nancy sighed inwardly, stepped back and waited for him to finish with the mail.

A few minutes later, Jonathon looked up and spying what Nancy was wearing looked surprised. "Are you going somewhere?"

Nancy paused for a second. "Aren't you taking me to dinner tonight?"

Jonathon thought for a moment and then remembered. "Oh, yeah! Dinner in Laguna Niguel. You know, the traffic's going to be a bitch. Could we go someplace closer, so we don't have to drive so far?"

"Oh. I was really looking forward to going to the beach. We haven't been out in ages and the girls are spending the night with friends, so we don't have any deadline." Nancy smiled with what she hoped was a come-hither smile.

Jonathon's mouth thinned out even more. "Okay. Give me a couple of minutes to change and we'll go." He left the kitchen without even giving her a peck on the cheek.

And that was the best part of the evening.

Jonathon spent the majority of the drive on his cell phone, working. At least it was a pretty drive, Nancy thought to herself as she watched the passing scenery.

When they arrived at the restaurant, the parking lot was already crowded. Nancy hoped that Jonathon would drop her off at the front door before he parked the car, but she didn't say anything and of course he didn't think of it. So she ended up walking across the parking lot in heels, which she rarely wore anymore.

They waited in the entry area for about fifteen minutes until their table was ready. They were then escorted to their table by the maître de, who held out Nancy's chair for her. Jonathon ordered a beer and Nancy ordered a glass of wine.

Between the time the waitress had taken their dinner orders and the food arrived, Jonathon asked Nancy,

"Have you given any thought to liposuction? It would be my anniversary gift to you." He even smiled while he said it.

Liposuction?!? What? Just last week a woman had died after liposuction! Would Jonathon rather have her dead than looking the way she did? She knew she'd put on 20 pounds with the babies, and sure hadn't been able to keep it off, even though she'd lost it several times, just to gain it back again.

But liposuction? Did she really look that bad?

Suddenly, Nancy felt old and ugly. She sure didn't have any appetite left. Perfect timing. The waitress brought the food.

Jonathon dug in and had been eating for several minutes when he looked up and noticed that Nancy wasn't eating.

"What's wrong?" Jonathon's brows came together over his nose.

"I'd like to go home. I don't feel like eating."

"Why?" Jonathon was thoroughly perplexed.

"I think you know why. I sure can't eat anything if you think I'm fat!" Nancy tried not to cry.

"Oh, for crying out loud, Nancy! I don't think you're necessarily fat, per se. I just thought you'd like to get some liposuction! I know you're not happy with the way you look right now and I thought you'd be pleased!" Jonathon was angry with her.

But Nancy just didn't care.

Jonathon had the waitress put their food in to-go boxes, he left a miserly tip, and they drove home in silence, much earlier than either of them had expected.

That night Nancy slept on the couch and neither she nor Jonathon ever brought up the subject of liposuction again.

He also never took her out again.

CHAPTER 13

"Hello! Earth to Mom!" Kate was smiling at Nancy.

Nancy came back to the present and looked at her hair in the mirror over the bathroom sink.

"Oh, honey! It's beautiful!" Kate had always had a way with hair and make-up. Nancy hoped she would use those talents in whatever profession she chose.

Nancy had no preconceived ideas about her children. All she wanted was for them to be happy and successful in whatever they decided to do.

Nancy glanced at the clock on the nightstand in her bedroom and gasped. "Oh! I've only got ten minutes!"

Just then, the doorbell rang.

"Make that zero seconds, Mom. Looks like your date is as anxious as you! I'll get the door." Kate went down the hall while Nancy put on her jewelry.

"Dad!" Kate's voice carried down the hallway.

Jonathon!?! What was HE doing here? And why NOW? Had she conjured him up by just thinking about him?

Nancy came out into the living room just as Jonathon and Kate were finishing a hug.

"Hi."

Jonathon turned around and paused when he saw Nancy. "You look good. Are you going somewhere?"

Nancy felt sucker punched. Jonathon sounded like he really meant she looked good -- for once.

"Mom has a date!" Kate was smiling at Jonathon. "Doesn't she look wonderful?"

Nancy frowned at Kate. What game was she playing?

Just then, the doorbell rang for a second time.

"I'll get it!" Nancy swung towards the door and beat Kate to it.

"Hi!" She smiled at Doug and opened the screen door so he could step into the house.

"You look great!" Doug was smiling into Nancy's eyes and Nancy was starting to feel that tingle again. Then he noticed Jonathon.

"Hi. I'm Jonathon." Jonathon stepped forward and held out his hand.

"Hi. I'm Doug." Doug shook Jonathon's hand and nodded.

The eye contact was palpable.

After an awkward pause where both men sized up the other, Nancy said "And we're leaving."

Since she was already holding her purse, she grabbed Doug's arm and turned towards the door.

"Wait. I needed to talk with you." Jonathon said.

"Now?" Nancy incredulously turned back and looked at Jonathon. He hadn't been by her house since the divorce and NOW he needed to talk?

And then Doug did the most wonderful thing. It wasn't a large move, but he shifted his weight closer to Nancy and rested his hand on the small of her back. Sort of like saying 'She's with me.' Doug's small motion made Nancy feel absolutely cherished and protected. It was thrilling.

Jonathon frowned at Doug then looked at Nancy. "Yeah. I got something from the IRS and I think it's for you." He handed an envelope to her. She looked at it a moment and then set it on the table next to the front door.

"Thank you for bringing it by, but you could have just mailed it." Nancy once again took Doug's arm and turned toward the door. "Bye, Kate. Don't wait up for me."

And with that the door closed behind her and Doug. She walked rapidly over to the motorcycle, grabbed the helmet he'd brought for her, and put it on. Doug followed suit and in no time they were on the road.

"Which movie theater are we going to?" Doug's voice carried back to Nancy.

Oh, Sugar! I forgot to pick out a movie! Nancy was embarrassed. "Doug. I'm sorry. I didn't get a chance to check what was playing. How about if we go to the Century Theatres? They always have a gazillion movies playing." She was able to make herself heard, even over the motorcycle engine.

"Sounds good!" And Doug headed out for Katella and Main. With his hand on her knee. Where it seemed to fit perfectly.

However, before they got to the theater, he pulled into the parking lot of the Katella Grill, a small local restaurant that had excellent food. When he stopped the bike, Nancy got off and looked at him with a question in her eyes.

"I don't know about you, but I'm starving!" Doug smiled and removed his helmet as he dismounted the bike. Nancy had her helmet off in seconds and ran her fingers through her hair, hoping against hope that Kate's good work wasn't in vain.

Their fingers brushed when Doug took Nancy's helmet and Nancy found herself trying to catch her breath while he secured the helmets to the back of the bike. He reached for Nancy's hand and walked with her to the front door of the restaurant. He opened the door with his other hand, but wouldn't let go of Nancy's, even though it was slightly awkward for her to move through the door and they both laughed.

The hostess seated them at a booth and instead of sliding in across from Nancy, Doug sat next to her still holding her hand. Nancy felt wonderful and gave Doug's hand a squeeze. Doug squeezed back, then turned his face to hers. They were only inches apart and their breaths mingled between them. Wow! He smelled good!

Doug felt his loins tighten and thought *'Oh boy, I'm in trouble, if only holding her hand does this to me!'*

They managed to get through dinner, and Doug sweet-talked the waitress into bringing them the movie section of that day's paper.

"Okay. It's a toss-up between the newest Bruce Willis movie *Die, Already* and the new Keanu Reeves movie where he's a cop again." Doug looked at Nancy expectantly.

"Wow. That's a tough choice. I like them both."

"Okay, we'll see both!" Doug slid out of the booth pulling Nancy behind him.

"Both! I've never done that. We won't get done until really late!" Nancy exclaimed.

Doug turned back to her and put his face a couple of inches from hers and said in a low husky voice, "You have a curfew, Miss?"

Nancy felt her stomach do flips. Oh, man, his eyes were gorgeous!

"Nope, no curfew, Officer."

Doug gave her a swift kiss, directly on the lips this time, and Nancy thought she'd never be able to catch her breath again. It felt so right every time he touched her. The kisses. The hand holding. His hand on her knee while they were on his bike. It felt natural.

Nancy really like the fact that Doug was so affectionate.

They parked right in front of the theater and after buying sodas, and popcorn, and Jordan Almonds, and red licorice, and a box of ice cream bonbons, they settled into their 5th row seats and waited for the Keanu Reeves movie to start.

Nancy had been surprised to discover that when it came to candy, Doug really enjoyed the palate of an 8-year old. It was actually quite endearing.

When Doug held up one of the bonbons to put in Nancy's mouth, Nancy shook her head "no."

Doug frowned, "Why not? I thought you liked ice cream."

"I do! In fact I like it TOO much. I'm trying to lose some weight, so I'm cutting out the sugar."

Doug popped the bon-bon into his own mouth, leaned down and gave Nancy a cold, ice-cream flavored kiss.

"I think you look perfect. You look like a mom and a woman. You're not built like a little boy. You've got curves. So sue me, I like curves, especially when they're on you."

Nancy looked into Doug's eyes, looking for the lie. She'd thought for so many years now that she was fat, and here was this extremely attractive male telling her she looked perfect. He dropped his eyes to her chest then looked back up and winked at her.

Then he reached into the bon-bon box, pulled out another one and held it to Nancy's lips. This time she opened her mouth and he gently placed the sweet inside. She closed her lips and chewed once, right before he leaned down and kissed her again. This time his tongue went across her lips and he made a yummy noise.

She thought she was going to melt right through the seat when the lights dimmed and the before-previews advertisements started. They reluctantly turned towards the screen and hunkered down in their seats.

They sat elbow to elbow and every time Doug reached into the popcorn box that was on Nancy's lap, the back of his arm brushed against her right breast. He kept his eyes glued to the screen and didn't seem to notice, but Nancy needed oxygen. She felt like a hot flash was going to happen any minute.

She handed the movie treats to Doug and excused herself for the ladies' room.

"Hurry back! You don't want to miss the previews. We'll figure out what we're gonna see next weekend." Doug smiled at her. From his smile, she knew that he knew exactly what he'd been doing to her.

Nancy's heart was racing a mile a minute and she just made it into the ladies room before the hot flash hit. Luckily it wasn't one of those that made her scalp wet, too. She rinsed her face and fluffed her hair.

While Nancy was in the bathroom, Doug sat in the theatre chewing popcorn as well as chewing over what he was doing. *Come on, man. Slow down or you'll scare her off. Yeah. Easy to say; hard to do. And speaking of hard.*

Doug adjusted himself by shifting in his seat and vowed to behave himself.

Nancy arrived back just in time for the previews and they decided they'd see the new Al Pacino movie next week. It looked entertaining.

Their first movie of the evening was fast-paced and full of "hero moments" for the good guy, who surprisingly wasn't Keanu Reeves! Instead, Keanu played the villain and did an excellent job.

However, when it got to the scene where he seduced the leading lady, both Doug and Nancy kept their eyes glued to the screen and didn't even touch elbows.

It would have been sensory overload.

That movie ended with the hero getting the girl.

The lights came up and they moved to the next theatre, showing the usher the second set of tickets they'd bought.

In the next movie, the Bruce Willis flick had something exploding every 3 or 4 minutes and was noisy and riveting.

See? Nancy thought during one close up of Mr. Willis. Bruce just keeps getting better and better with age even though he's lost so much hair that he'd shaved his head. He's sweating, he's dirty and he's hot. Yes, he's hot. And Doug's very hot. And so was she ... again. Damn, another flash.

She used one of the napkins and tried to wipe her face without Doug noticing. Fat chance of that. They'd been tuned into each other all evening like sonar in a submarine tuned into a torpedo coming straight at the sub.

He looked at her questioningly when he saw in the light from the screen that Nancy was perspiring and looked uncomfortable.

"Are you all right?" He'd leaned close and whispered into her ear. All that did was make her hotter.

"I'm fine. I'll be right back." Nancy escaped into the ladies room for the second time that evening and waited for the redness under her skin to go away. Her doctor had said that she should avoid spicy foods, coffee and alcohol if she wanted to lessen the symptoms of her hot flashes. Too bad the doctor hadn't also mentioned sitting too close to a very attractive male!

Nancy used a wet paper towel with a little bit of soap to wipe her upper chest and neck and down both her arms. She then wet another towel and washed the back of her neck, hoping to cool herself off. Maybe she would go back to the doctor and ask about the hormone replacement prescription.

She finally slid back into her seat and smiled at Doug. He smiled back and took her right hand and slid it through his left elbow. They snuggled in their seats and sat that way for the remainder of the movie -- of which neither of them could have remembered the ending if you'd offered them a million dollars to do so. They were only aware of each other.

When the movie ended, they walked hand in hand out to the lobby after depositing their trash into a bin. Another thing they had in common.

They put on their helmets and rode home. The long way. It was great. His hand on her knee. The soft wind. The full moon. The smell of orange blossoms from the groves they drove past. Nancy felt like she was 18 again.

All too soon, they arrived at Nancy's house. She got off the bike, took off her helmet and handed it to Doug once he was off the bike.

"Keep it. Actually I bought it for you." Doug looked down at his feet and then back at Nancy.

"How sweet! Thank you. I shouldn't accept it, but I like it too much to refuse. Besides, it'll give me a chance to practice with my hair and the helmet to see what works."

By this point, they'd arrived at her front door.

She felt Doug's hand on her shoulder and turned to face him. "Thank you, Doug. I had a wonderful time." Nancy stood on her toes and gave him a kiss on the side of his mouth.

As she was pulling away, she felt his arms go around her and pull her to him.

Looking down into her face, Doug huskily said "I'm sorry, Nancy. I promised myself I'd be good tonight. But I can't help it."

With that declaration, he groaned like he'd given up and his lips descended upon hers, his left arm tightened around her back and his right hand moved up to cup the back of her head, tipping her head to the side, while he drank from her mouth.

After dropping the helmet in surprise, Nancy could only cling to his shoulders. There was no way her knees were going to support her. Thankfully, his arms did.

After a momentary hesitation, she kissed him back with everything she had. He felt so right. She wanted to climb inside of him. They couldn't seem to get close enough.

It had been so long since she'd been kissed like this, and he felt so good! The contrast between his soft lips and the slight scratchiness of his 5:00 shadow was exhilarating. Very male.

Without lifting his mouth, Doug moved Nancy until her back came up against the alcove wall next to the front door and he plastered himself against her so that chest met breast, abdomen met stomach, and his right thigh moved between hers.

The kiss deepened until Nancy thought she'd shatter from the sensations flowing through her. She was sure their combined heat was going to cause smoke!

Suddenly she found herself alone, leaning against the wall with Doug standing in front of her, holding his hands out to his sides and taking deep breaths.

She didn't trust herself to stand on her own feet. She was also trying to find her breath.

Doug's eyes had turned deep black and were smoldering with passion. He placed his hands flat on his thighs as though trying to keep himself from reaching for her again.

Nancy took a deep breath and then launched herself at Doug. This time they ended up with HIS back against the opposite wall and her right thigh between his.

Again his lips descended and devoured Nancy's. Their heads tipped side to side while their lips released and sealed, again and again.

Doug thought he'd go mad when Nancy's tongue touched the tip of his. He reached down and pulled her jeans up tight against his. He groaned when Nancy lifted her thigh. He knew for sure he had to end this kiss now, or he'd end up pulling her to the mat in front of her door.

He put his hands on her shoulders and gently placed her away from him. Nancy's lips were swollen and moist. Her eyes were heavy lidded and there was a very becoming flush in her cheeks.

Doug bet that wasn't all of Nancy's that was swollen, moist and flushed, if his own body was any indication. *Cool it, man! Or she'll NEVER go out with you again!*

Nancy's eyes came back into focus and she just stared at Doug. Then it dawned on her how brazenly she'd just plastered herself against him! She swiftly turned towards her front door, searching in her purse for her keys, embarrassed beyond belief.

While bending her head down, she suddenly felt soft breath on the nape of her neck. Oh, no! Not the neck! She'd never be able to behave herself if he…

Too late.

Doug's mouth dropped to the exposed back of Nancy's neck and he put small soft kisses all along the back of it. His mouth reached the top of her spine and his tongue flicked out to taste her neck.

That was Nancy's undoing. Did he have any idea what that did to her? It had been so long since anyone had touched her there, and he did it so well. So softly, so gently, with an underlying urgency that made her knees go weak.

His left arm came around from the back and for once she didn't even think of her stomach when his hand splayed across her abdomen pulling her up against his front. It just felt right. She could feel his heat through the back of her jeans.

He continued to make love to the back of her neck and Nancy was sure that she'd never again be able to see straight, much less walk.

Just then the porch light blazed on and both Doug and Nancy felt like they'd been doused with a bucket of cold water. They jumped apart and were standing once again facing each other when the front door opened.

"Oh, it's you." Christy was yawning and scratching her head. "I thought it was Jackson. He had to work late and …" Her voice trailed off when she finally looked at her mom and Doug. Wow that must have been some necking party! Mom looked guilty and Doug looked … well he looked frustrated. Yep, good thing Christy had come to the door when she had.

Christy tried to keep the smile from her face while she opened the screen door for her mom. "Wow! Did you get a new helmet?" Christy pretended to not see the look that passed between Doug and her mom when he picked the helmet off the ground and handed it to Nancy.

Her mom, making out. Go figure. You think she still gets the hots? Sure looks like it.

Nancy turned around and extended her hand to Doug. "Thank you for the wonderful evening."

Doug reached out and took Nancy's hand. With Christy standing right there, there wasn't much else he could say or do. He leaned in and kissed Nancy on the cheek, his breath tickling her ear. "Sleep well."

With that he dropped her hand, said goodnight to Christy and walked back to his bike. Good thing it was dark or Christy would guess what he and her mom had been up to. He took his time putting on his helmet so that he'd be able to throw his leg over the bike and sit down on the seat in reasonable comfort.

Closing the door behind them, Christy said, "You want something to eat before you go to bed, Mom?"

"No thanks sweetie. I'm pretty tired. I think I'll just go to bed." *And lie awake tossing and turning in frustration all night!*

Nancy said good night and went down the hall to her bedroom. She didn't even turn on the light. She just stripped while heading for the bed, dropping clothes in her wake, slid between the sheets and pulled the covers over her head. She could still taste Doug and smell him. She thought she'd never be able to fall asleep, but surprisingly her fatigue won out and she was asleep before she knew it ... dreaming a really great dream.

CHAPTER 14

"So, how was your date, Mom?"

"Huh?" Nancy had just put oatmeal in the coffee maker and hazelnut flavored coffee grounds into a saucepan on the stove.

"That good, huh?" Kate laughed and put her hands on Nancy's shoulders and steered her into a chair in the breakfast nook. "Sit."

Kate went over to the coffee maker and the stove and switched everything to where it was supposed to be.

When the coffee was ready, she brought Nancy her cup of coffee and sat down across from her with her own.

"So. How was the movie?"

After taking a sip, Nancy replied almost normally, "We saw two!"

"Two! No wonder you got home so late."

Nancy glanced at Kate. "What time did I get home?"

"Christie said around 1:30 in the morning! Good thing it was a Friday night, so you could sleep late this morning."

Kate got up and put the cooked oatmeal into two bowls and brought them to the table, placing one in front of Nancy and one at her seat.

Then she brought over brown sugar, butter and cream, plus two spoons.

Nancy fixed her oatmeal in silence and Kate waited patiently for her to speak.

After several moments of silence Nancy cleared her throat.

"Hon?"

"Yeah, Mom?"

Nancy looked like she was going to say more, but then turned her attention back to the oatmeal and ate ... and smiled.

They sat that way for quite a while, just eating their oatmeal and drinking their coffee.

"Mom?"

"Yeah, Hon?"

"If you ever want to talk, I'm here."

Nancy smiled into Kate's eyes and felt thankful for the gift of her wonderful girls. "I know that, Hon. Thank you."

"You're welcome, Mom," Kate mumbled around a mouthful of oatmeal.

The rest of the weekend was spent in a sort of happy haze for Nancy, especially when Doug called Saturday night just to talk while he had a lull at work.

Nancy thought it was wonderful that they could talk so freely about so many different subjects. Even the times when they disagreed on something, there was no acrimony involved.

She was really starting to fall for Doug.

After they hung up the phone, (and after Doug had asked Nancy what she was wearing to bed!) Doug found that he couldn't stop thinking about Nancy.

As Patty and Bill had so fondly pointed out to him, Nancy sure wasn't his usual type. But that's what made her so special to him. He could picture himself living with her for the rest of his life, growing old together.

The thought made Doug smile, and not even a belligerent drunk who spit on him when he had to arrest the man took away the warm feeling.

....

"So, how was your date?"

"Huh?" Doug had to unlock his locker – again. This time in order to get out his utility belt and cap.

"That good, huh?" Bill laughed putting on his own belt and waited for Doug to retrieve his.

It was now Monday at 2:00 pm and Bill hadn't been able to get two words out of Doug about his date with Nancy last Friday night. All Doug had said was that it was "good."

"Well, what the heck does THAT mean?" Patty had wanted to know.

"Hell if I know, Sweetie. That's all he said." Bill was almost as determined to find out as his wife was.

"Bring him home for dinner tonight. I'll find out." Patty assured her husband.

"Okay." Bill gave her a kiss on the cheek and a pat on one of the lower ones and left the house whistling. Patty smiled and closed the door behind him. Boy, for being married so long, they still enjoyed each other. Bill was the first man she'd ever made love to, and gods willing, the last.

Patty went into the kitchen and looking through her freezer and cupboards, decided they'd grill steaks for dinner. Add a tossed spinach salad, garlic bread and a "Death By Chocolate" cake for dessert, and Doug wouldn't be able to withstand any of her questions.

Now Bill was sitting next to Doug in the ready room and told him that Patty was expecting him for dinner that night.

To Bill's surprise, Doug readily accepted.

"Well, good! Be at the house by 9:00. We're eating late tonight."

"Count on it." Doug put on his cap and sunglasses and headed for his unit.

While cruising around his assigned section, Doug's thoughts kept coming back to Nancy and last Friday night.

This was becoming more than just an infatuation and Doug knew it. Although he'd dated some of the most beautiful women in Orange County, he'd never felt so many different feelings for one woman in his entire life. He felt protective, tender, happy, charmed, and above all whenever he was within 10 feet of her, his hands itched to touch her. Doug thought he was starting to understand part of Nancy's appeal. She didn't wear blatantly sexy clothes. She didn't walk into a room expecting all the men to turn and look at her. Instead, her attention was on him; and when she looked at him with those wide green eyes she made him feel like he could accomplish anything in the whole world. Her soft, curvy body was made to fit in his arms. And she smelled so good! Other women he'd dated had worn expensive perfume and he was sure they'd gone to spas once or twice a week. Yet here was Nancy with her work-roughened hands and auburn hair with a few strands of silver starting to come in at the crown of her head. Doug smiled to himself as he wondered if Nancy even knew the strands were there. He found he was more attracted to Nancy than he'd been to anyone else he'd ever known.

Her good heart was also a major part of the attraction. She easily saw the best in others. There were few people that Doug had found in the world who didn't criticize others. Nancy was one of those few people. That didn't mean she couldn't hold her own when it came to her kids. She just didn't stick up for herself the way Doug thought she deserved. That was all right. He was here now to do it for her. And hopefully in return, she'd save him from a lonely existence.

Doug smiled as he pictured Nancy and himself sitting side by side on a front porch somewhere, with a dozen grandkids running around. Her face would still be showing her emotions and lighting up her eyes, just as they did now. Nice picture.

CHAPTER 15

"Ms. Adams. Could I see you a moment, please?" The principal, Victoria stuck her head into Nancy's classroom about three minutes before the final bell that Monday.

"Certainly, Mrs. Newman. Coming." Nancy got up from her desk and told her students to finish cleaning up and she'd be right back.

She stepped out into the hall and was accosted by a tropical rainforest. Actually it was a very large bouquet which must have cost a small fortune!

Nancy just stared with her mouth hanging open.

"It's for you, Nancy!" Mrs. Newman was smiling while the school secretary held the bouquet.

"Why, thank you! Whatever for?" Nancy accepted the bouquet in the gorgeous green vase.

"You'll have to read the card to find out, I suppose. They just arrived and we're all dying to find out who they're from!" The principal and her secretary stood there waiting for Nancy to do just that.

"Oh! I thought they were from you." Nancy said embarrassed.

"Will you open the card for pity's sake?" The school secretary was not big on patience.

They followed Nancy into her classroom and waited as she put the bouquet on her desk while her students oo'ed and aw'ed.

A slight smile started to form on her mouth as she opened the card.

The card was hand printed in block letters, like a cop would use on a report sheet.

You take my breath away.

That's all it said. No salutation, no signature.

Nancy had trouble catching HER breath. She handed the card to Mrs. Newman. The principal read the card, blushed and handed it to the secretary, who in turn read it and also got red.

"Who's it from, Ms. Adams?" Tess called out from the back of the room where she was helping clean up.

"There's no signature," Nancy replied.

"Hm-m-m. Must be that police officer." Tess winked at Nancy just as the bell rang for the end of the day.

"Which police officer?" Mrs. Newman asked as the students piled out of the room.

"That one." Tess pointed at the door where Doug stood in all his uniformed splendor amid a sea of exiting backs.

Nancy smiled into Doug's eyes and he smiled back at her across the room.

You could have cut through the heat radiating between them. Tess, Mrs. Newman and the school secretary all mumbled something about "nice flowers" and "good-bye" as they left the room past Doug.

He stayed at the doorway, even after the door had closed behind him. Nancy stayed next to her desk holding the card from the bouquet.

They smiled at each other across the room, and Doug started to walk slowly towards her.

"I sure hope these are from you, or I'm in trouble with the science teacher," Nancy teased.

"What science teacher?" Doug pretended to glower.

"You know. The short bald one who's been asking me out." Nancy's smile got wider.

"Well, I'll just have to have a word with him. Sending flowers to my girl." Doug stopped walking. "You are my girl, right?"

Nancy started walking towards Doug. "Yep. There's something about a man wearing Kevlar that I just can't resist." Nancy said as she moved close and put her palms against Doug's chest.

Doug looked down at her hands and sighed, "I am wearing entirely too much clothing right now."

"Not at all," Nancy breathed. "You feel great." Nancy flexed her fingers.

Just then Doug snaked an arm out and pinned Nancy up against his chest. "You realize, Ma'am, you're taking the law into your own hands here."

Nancy groaned and leaned her forehead against Doug's body armor. "That was terrible, Saunders." She looked back up and smiled into his face.

Doug started to lower his lips to hers but she stepped back while putting both arms out straight with her hands flat against his chest.

"Huh-uh! No monkey business in my classroom. A student could walk in at any moment!"

Doug was reaching for her again with a grin on his lips when his radio crackled. "Excuse me a second," he smiled at Nancy, holding her eyes with his, while he reached up to his left lapel to speak into the mike.

"Saunders, here. Go ahead."

The radio squawked again and Doug's face frowned.

"Say, again?"

Once again the radio cracked and squeaked and Nancy heard something that sounded like "domestic in progress."

"Ten-four. On my way."

"I'm sorry. I've got to go." Doug leaned down and gave Nancy a quick husband-like kiss. "I'll call you later."

"Okay," Nancy replied to the closing door of her classroom. She hoped the call wasn't anything terrible.

That evening, Nancy fretted a bit, since she hadn't heard from Doug and had actually assumed she'd be seeing him. She'd taken the time for a luxurious bubble bath and had attended to her personal grooming beyond the usual. She'd even painted her toenails with the soft Angel Hair pink that Kate had used on her nails earlier that week.

But by the time 11:00 pm rolled around, she decided that she should just go to bed. Nancy walked into the kitchen to make sure everything was turned off and locked up when she looked though her window and spotted a black and white unit sitting in the driveway.

It was Doug!

She ran back to her bedroom, grabbed her robe and sailed out the front door and over to the driver's side of the unit.

When Doug saw Nancy flying out the front door towards him, his heart tripped into double time. He'd wanted to call her earlier, but hadn't wanted to burden her with the awful afternoon he'd had.

Suddenly she was there next to his open window, and a soft breeze carried the slight scent of spring rain to him. He'd come to love the way she smelled, and looked, and talked, and, well he loved just about everything about her.

She put a hand on his left shoulder.

"Doug? Are you okay?" Nancy's voice sounded wonderful.

He cleared his throat around the obstruction that had lodged there around 4:00 pm that afternoon and hadn't yet moved.

"Not really. Do you have a minute?"

"Of course! Do you want to come in?"

"No. I'd rather stay in the car. Come around to the other side and I'll let you in there."

Nancy walked around to the passenger side of the car while Doug leaned across and pushed open the door for her.

She slid into the seat, adjusted her robe around her, looked over at Doug and waited. She knew he'd tell her what had happened without any prompting from her.

God! He loved that about her. Her calmness. Her utter calmness and patience. He hadn't planned on burdening her with the day's events, but he truly felt the need to express his feelings to someone.

He needed a friend. He needed a wife. Looking over at Nancy in that faded bathrobe and looking so feminine in spite of it, Doug knew that tonight was a test. If Nancy could handle what he going to tell her, then she'd be able to handle his life.

Oh, how he hoped she could handle it.

PAT ADEFF

CHAPTER 16

When Doug left Nancy's classroom earlier that afternoon, his mind was only half on the job. The other half was taken up with where he would take Nancy that night and then what he'd do once he got his arms around her.

She sure liked the Kevlar vest! It was scratchy and hot, but now he'd found a second use for it ... getting Nancy hot!

Doug headed to the address he'd been given by the dispatcher with lights flashing and sirens screaming. He hoped that Bill would be one of the other units for back-up.

No one on the force looked forward to answering domestic disturbance calls. You just never knew how crazy they were going to be. One time, Doug had stepped in and stopped a drunk from beating his wife; only to have the wife attack his back while he was handcuffing the husband! Weird.

He pulled up in front of the seedy apartment complex, got out of his unit, and locked it. Nowadays he couldn't leave the unit without locking it. A few years ago, one of his fellow officers had responded to a call, left the vehicle unattended for less than two minutes and had come back to find his rifle, computer, and various other items missing. Of course, no one had seen anything and no one knew anything either.

Now it was just standard procedure to secure the unit.

Doug heard the yelling and screaming coming from the second floor apartment as he moved between the people who had gathered on the lawn to watch. He entered the building and was first on the scene and consequently the first one to approach the second floor landing.

As he rounded the top of the stairwell, Doug had his gun holster unbuckled and his right hand rested on the gun's handle.

"Police!" Doug yelled loud enough to be heard over the fight that was coming from apartment 206.

The sound of breaking glass and a woman's scream sent his heart rate up 40 beats a minute. However to the casual observer Doug would have appeared unaffected.

He moved closer to the door just as Officer O'Connor arrived on the landing. Doug nodded at Diane and she let him know with a return nod that she was ready whenever he was.

Diane drew her gun and kept it pointed at the floor. Doug approached the door from the side and gave it three hard swift knocks.

"Orange Police! Open the door!" Although Doug's voice was loud enough to carry down the stairs and outside, he still sounded calm and cool.

Just then the center of the door exploded outward from a shotgun that had been fired from inside the apartment.

Doug rapidly drew his gun and crouched at the side of the door. Diane plastered herself against the hallway wall and used her lapel mike to call for backup and announce "shots fired."

Suddenly the remainder of the door was flung open from the inside and a man came stumbling out like he was drunk. Although that might have also been the case, the man was holding his hands to what was left of his face. From Doug's perspective, all he could see was a bloody mess where there should have been eyes, a nose and a mouth.

The opening that should have had lips and teeth gaped open and a high keening animal sound emitted from it.

The man then fell to the floor unconscious and stayed that way.

The only sound in the hallway was the ringing left over from the spent gun and Diane's calm voice calling for paramedics.

Doug took a deep fortifying breath and called into the apartment. The tangy copper smell of fresh blood coated his throat and nose. He knew from experience it would take a long time to get the taste out.

"Put the gun down on the floor outside the doorway, and come out with your hands on top of your head. Move slowly."

Doug heard a whimpering sound from inside the apartment and the sound of metal when the gun was dropped on the faded linoleum doorstep.

He watched as a small haggard looking woman stepped over the gun and out into the hallway with her hands on top of her head. She was dirty with stringy hair that looked greasy and knotted. Her face looked battered. He could smell her from six feet away.

When she saw her husband on the floor, she crumbled to the ground and started sobbing, her shoulders shaking. "He just wouldn't stop hitting me. I begged him to stop, but he wouldn't."

Just then Bill and another officer arrived on the scene. Doug and Diane exchanged looks and Doug entered the apartment with his gun drawn while Diane and Bill cuffed the woman and checked the man for a pulse. He had one.

It was a small dirty apartment with a kitchenette and a cramped bathroom. There was a 12 foot by 12 foot main room which did double duty as the living room and the bedroom.

Doug quickly ascertained that the apartment held no more dangers and was about to holster his gun when he heard what he thought was a small cat mewling from what seemed to be an old clothes hamper in the corner of the bathroom.

Keeping his hand on his gun, Doug opened the top of the hamper.

Looking up from inside the dirty chamber was an infant. The only thing it had on was a very old diaper which was wet as well as soiled. Its arms and legs were covered in flea bites and open sores. Its eyes were shadowed and dry. Its mouth was barely working, only putting out a small sound that was more like an inhuman whimper.

"Oh my God!" Diane said from behind Doug's right shoulder. "Oh my God!" she repeated as she reached down to gather up the infant.

Doug tried to stop her with a hand to her shoulder. "Diane, wait for the paramedics."

"No way, Saunders. This baby needs immediate attention." She made cooing noises while she gathered the small frail thing in her arms and it stopped making its whimper for a moment, just looking at her with its hollow eyes.

Diane's eyes misted over and Doug had to turn away and clear his throat several times before he could trust himself to speak. He could hear Bill speaking to the woman out in the hall.

Just then the room lit up with paramedics and more cops and Doug found himself backed into the kitchenette. He looked around at the counter top and saw drug paraphernalia littered all over the place. The two grimy baby bottles that were in the sink appeared to have clotted formula in them.

Doug turned around in time to see one of the paramedics gently taking the infant out of Diane's arms and placing it on a stretcher which dwarfed it even further.

There was a hush that was almost reverent.

"It's a little girl" one of the paramedics said in a soft voice when he removed the filthy rag that was serving as her diaper, replacing it with a clean absorbent pad.

Doug could hear the woman now out in the hallway screaming "Gloria! Don't let them take my Gloria."

He also heard Bill's voice say "They'll take good care of her ma'am." Doug knew that if Bill could see the shape the infant was in, that he wouldn't have even answered the woman, he would be so disgusted.

Finally the husband and the child were transported to the county hospital and the woman was taken into custody after the paramedics checked out her face which had a small laceration above a very large bruise on her right cheek. There were other assorted bruises which varied in depth and color, indicating that she'd received them at earlier times.

Both she and her husband had multiple track marks from needles going up and down their arms and legs. The woman even had marks between her toes.

Doug looked around the apartment one last time before leaving and turning it over to the detectives who would secure the door and plaster crime scene tape across it to keep nosy neighbors out.

As he went back to his unit he spied Diane leaning against her unit talking with another officer, her fiancé. Doug didn't want to intrude, although he could sure use some human company that wasn't degraded and dirty.

He thought once again about going over and speaking with Diane, but she and Mike were intent in their conversation and lost to the rest of the world. So Doug got into his black and white and drove back to the station to fill out the requisite forms. He could have done them in his car, but he needed the safe, sane space of the precinct and his fellow officers around him.

CHAPTER 17

Doug finally finished up the paperwork from the domestic disturbance case. It was 8:00 pm but he wasn't tired. He was still running on adrenaline aftermath and when Sergeant Peters asked him to cover another shift since they were down two guys, he agreed. Besides he could use the extra pay. Christmas was coming in six weeks.

Now here he was, driving up and down the dark streets of Orange. It was one of those rare times where everyone was in their home for the night. Occasionally he saw a small group of gang bangers, but as soon as they spotted him, they scattered like roaches when the light gets turned on.

There wasn't even a drunken fight at any of the local bars. It was an eerily quiet night.

Doug felt antsy and itchy. He felt agitated. He knew that the baby today had affected him more than he wanted to admit. Why didn't people cherish what was given to them? He needed to talk, but he wasn't sure who to turn to. The abused infant made his thoughts turn to the son he hadn't helped raise. He'd respected Sue's request, but still wished he'd done more. That was it. Maybe he'd go talk to Sue about it. She'd been a cop. She'd understand. Doug felt so confused.

Doug pulled up in front of Sue's house and walked up to the door. He rang the doorbell and waited.

Finally he heard the deadbolt turning. Instead of seeing Sue, he saw a male he didn't recognize.

"Can I help you?" The guy's tone was just this side of rude. He was also parading in his boxers and looked like he'd just gotten out of bed.

"Who is it, Sam?" Doug could hear Sue's voice from down the hall.

"It's a cop." said in the same tone of voice someone would use to announce the plague. Sam stepped away from the door when Sue, gathering her kimono wrapper around her, came to the door.

"Doug! I didn't expect to see you! What are you doing here?" Sue seemed pleased to see him, but puzzled.

"Ah. Hey there, Sue. Is Andy here?" Doug lied. He wouldn't know what to say to Andy, but Doug suddenly knew that talking to Sue wasn't what he needed.

"No, Doug. He's out with friends." Sue waited patiently for a reply.

"Oh, okay. When he gets back, tell him I stopped by. Sorry to have bothered you, Sue. Good night." Doug backed down off the step and turned back to his unit.

He heard the door close behind him right after he heard Sam say "Come on, baby. Close the door. It's cold."

Now he was cruising down Katella and realized he was just a couple of blocks from Nancy's house. Nancy. It would be very good to see her. But it was so late. And he wasn't sure he wanted to contaminate her life with what he'd been submerged in that afternoon.

Doug convinced himself that if he went there and the lights were off, he'd just drive past without stopping. *Please have your lights on, Nancy. I really need to talk to you tonight.*

Now he was sitting in the driveway of Nancy's house and she was sitting just a foot away from him. Smelling clean and fresh and looking soft and pretty.

He'd told her everything that had happened and she hadn't said a word, except to clarify what he'd said here and there so that she could fully understand.

Some time during the dissertation, she'd taken his right hand and had held it softly between hers.

Somehow she'd mended the hurt. Now she leaned across the console that rested between them and kissed Doug softly on the jaw.

"Would you like to come in?"

Her invitation included much more than just coffee and they both knew it.

Doug was so tempted to bury himself in her arms and forget about the rest of the world.

However, this wasn't how he'd planned the first time they made love. Oh, he'd thought about it for hours all right, but tonight was not going to be that night.

He looked down into her eyes and then gently kissed her. "No. Not tonight."

Somehow Nancy understood that he wasn't rejecting her offer. He was just postponing it.

He kissed her again, this time drinking from her mouth and making her moan.

"You sure you don't want to rethink my offer, Saunders?" Nancy sounded breathless and sexy.

"I must be some sort of fool. But the answer is still going to be no for tonight. Can I take a rain check?" He smiled as he dipped down for another lingering kiss.

"I'll have you know I'm not the local department store on sale day. No rain checks allowed. And I'm not sure the offer will still stand tomorrow." Nancy was teasing him and he loved it.

"Well then, we'll just have to wait until the perfect time, won't we?" Doug wasn't sure when that would be, but he sure knew it wasn't tonight, although Nancy was cute enough to tempt the devil sitting there in the front seat of his black and white in her robe . . . and no slippers.

"Hon! You don't even have slippers on. Aren't you freezing?" Doug hadn't even noticed that she'd come to him barefoot.

"They're just slightly cold. Not that bad." Nancy rubbed her right foot to warm it up.

"Wait right there." Doug got out of the driver's side and rounded the front of the unit. He opened the passenger door and leaned in and lifted Nancy into his arms.

"Doug! Put me down. You'll hurt your back!" Nancy was half mortified and half excited. No one had carried her since that one summer in high school when the lifeguard she had a crush on at the pool was fooling around flirting with her and had picked her up and thrown her into the deep end. He'd ruined her hair and make-up, but she'd floated on air for the rest of that summer whenever she thought about how he'd then jumped in after her. She sure was a sucker for heroes.

Doug shifted Nancy in his arms so she was more settled and just stood there holding her.

Their eyes met and Nancy was certain that he was going to change his mind about coming in. Doug carried her to the front door porch and set her down gently, releasing her feet first. Of course, he made sure that she slid down his chest for a good portion of the time he was releasing her.

Just about every fantasy that Nancy had was rolled up in this one man. He was handsome. He was gentle. He was sexy. He was a hero. And he really seemed to care about her. Of course, it didn't hurt that he was also wearing Kevlar and a gun belt.

Doug leaned down and kissed Nancy on the nose.

"Goodnight, sweetheart. Catch you later." He backed away from her with his hands behind his back as though keeping himself from reaching for her again.

"So what are you going to do now?" Nancy was breathless just watching him walk.

"Take a very long cold shower."

Nancy could hear Doug's laughter as he pulled out of her driveway and drove down the street.

It wasn't until she could no longer hear him that she realized she was standing on her front porch wearing just a robe and oversized tee shirt under it.

Her feet WERE cold!

She turned and quietly entered her house. She softly shut the door and latched the lock. Then she turned around… and screamed.

Her heart stuttered to a stop and then drove itself into a spectacular rendition of the Anvil Chorus.

"Hey! Mom Adams! It's me. Jackson! Geez! You scared the sh… stuff out of me!" Jackson was backed against the entry hall wall with both his hands to his chest.

Just then, both Kate and Christy came running to the front door from their respective bedrooms, yelling "Mom!" "Jackson!"

Nancy felt a nervous bubble of laughter rising in her throat and was afraid that if she let it go, she'd end up sounding hysterical. Too late. The giggle came out of her mouth against all her wishes.

Well once Nancy's laughter started, then Jackson's did. Then Kate and Christy chimed in. The four of them ended up laughing so hard, they slid to the floor in glee. Just about the time they thought the hilarity was drawing to a close, one of them would make eye contact with another, and off they went again.

It finally died down enough that they were able to get themselves off the floor.

"Anyone hungry?" Nancy asked the group of young people.

"Always." Jackson answered with such a tone of mournfulness in his voice that it started them all off again in peals of laughter.

Nancy grabbed bowls and spoons while the girls got out the ice cream and chocolate sauce from the refrigerator.

Jackson was now sitting quietly at the table, which got Nancy to thinking.

"Jackson? What were you doing in the hall way?"

Jackson and Christy sneaked looks at each other and then got very busy making their sundaes.

Nancy realized with a start that it was probably way past the time she should have had "the talk" with her girls. While they were growing up, she'd always answered all their questions honestly; but she'd never brought up the subject of sex herself.

Now she just looked at the kids.

"I assume you were going home." Nancy tried hard to make her voice sound normal. Christy and Kate were old enough to have boyfriends. She also knew that they both could think for themselves and she found she wasn't worried.

Jackson cleared his throat and looked at Nancy. "Mom Adams, I've been wanting to talk with you."

Christy grabbed Jackson's hand. "Not now, babe. Later."

"Not now what, honey?" Now Nancy was curious.

Jackson looked intently at Christy until she finally nodded 'OK.'

"Mom Adams. I'd like to ask for Christy's hand in marriage."

Nancy's mouth dropped open in surprise. Boy she hadn't seen that one coming. Well, at least not yet.

"Jackson." Nancy pulled her thoughts together because she knew how important this conversation was.

"Jackson. I'm honored that you'd ask me. And thank you for that. However, Christy makes her own decisions and can give you her hand herself."

"Well, Mom," Christy spoke up. "We want your blessing and approval."

"Of course you have that, Honey! Jackson is a wonderful man. You make a great couple."

Christy turned to Jackson. "See? Didn't I tell you she'd understand?"

Jackson just nodded and smiled.

Nancy looked over at Kate and noticed that she was drawing patterns in her melted ice cream and chocolate sauce.

Nancy made eye contact with Christy who just shrugged her shoulders.

"Kate? Honey? You okay?"

"What? Oh, sure. Sure! Congratulations you guys! This is awesome."

Kate's metamorphosis was so complete that Nancy would have doubted that anything was troubling her. Except that she knew her daughter pretty well.

Nancy made a mental note to have a heart-to-heart with Kate as soon as they were alone. And it wasn't after midnight.

It only took everyone a couple of minutes to clean up the bowls and spilled ice cream. Jackson kissed Christy goodnight and left on his motorcycle.

She gave both her girls a goodnight hug and they all went to bed.

As Nancy snuggled down under the covers on her bed, she again thought about how Doug had come to her tonight and told her about his day. It felt wonderful. He seemed to need her as much as she needed him. They balanced each other.

She also really liked the way he'd carried her to the door. Just the way he'd looked at her made her wish she'd been wearing better sleepwear. Maybe she should go shopping.

Chapter 18

"A tuxedo! A penguin suit? No way."

"Come on, Doug! You'll look great in it." Patty was determined to meet Nancy and this was the only way she knew how. "All you need to do is stand up and propose a toast. I'll even write it for you. It couldn't be easier."

Doug had absolutely no recollection of having agreed to being Bill's Best Man when Bill and Patty renewed their wedding vows. In fact, he didn't even remember Bill saying anything about any ceremony.

Doug turned to Bill for support, but Bill suddenly found his cup of coffee to be extremely interesting and wouldn't let Doug catch his eye. Bill had stayed married as long as he had with good reason. He knew when to stay out of the way and let Patty do whatever it was she was determined to do. And right now he honestly was clueless about what Patty was saying. A ceremony?

They were having a postponed dinner of steak, salad and chocolate cake. Since Doug hadn't been able to make it the previous evening, Patty had insisted on him coming for dinner tonight.

Her idea of a vows renewal was one of her typical on-the-spot ideas. Surprisingly, most of her best ideas were off the cuff.

"Bill! When did you guys decide to do this?" Doug was half perplexed, half perturbed. He cursed himself for having the sneaking suspicion that Patty was doing all this just to meet Nancy.

"Uh, Dear? When did we decide this?" Bill turned a bland face to his wife.

"Oh, you remember, Honey. It was way back last summer some time. Remember?" Patty had on one of her patented sweet smiles.

"Of course, last summer. See, Doug? Last summer." Bill went back to perusing his coffee cup.

"So, how come I hadn't heard of it before now?" Doug was not going to be easily swayed.

"You did!" Patty even said it with what appeared to be an earnest look.

"When?"

"Last summer! In fact, we were sitting right here, weren't we, Bill." She continued to toss the salad.

"Yes, Dear."

"See, Doug! Even Bill says it's true."

Doug rolled his eyes and kept his mouth shut.

"Salad?"

"Yes, please, Patty." Doug knew when he was beat.

"By the way…"

Doug braced himself for what he just knew was coming next.

"Why don't you invite your new lady friend. What was her name?" Patty should have been on the stage.

"Nancy Adams." Doug was starting to find this whole conversation somewhat comical.

"Right! Nancy. Do you think she'd be able to attend?" Patty put baked potatoes on each of their plates.

"I imagine she would. When is the ceremony?"

"Next Saturday."

At that announcement, both men turned to Patty and just stared with their mouths open.

Patty didn't miss a beat. "Since it's only family and very close friends, it will be somewhat informal."

"Then why the tux?"

"For the photos, of course." Patty poured more coffee into their cups.

....

Nancy was thrilled and appalled at the same time. She was meeting Doug's best friends – which was good. However, she only had one week to find a suitable dress and shoes, get a haircut, manicure (time for a facial?) to make herself presentable.

What would they think of her? Would they approve? She hoped so.

Doug had just stopped by after school and asked if she'd be his date for the event. He seemed slightly reluctant, which made her nervous. However, he'd picked up on her nervousness and had explained that this was Patty's way of finally meeting Nancy. He then explained his real reason for the reluctance – the tuxedo. At that, Nancy had laughed and told him that she was sure he'd be the most handsome guy there. Doug then explained that except for Bill, his two sons, and the minister, he'd be the only other guy there.

When Nancy looked puzzled, Doug explained that it was going to be a very small, intimate ceremony.

"Then why the tux?"

"The pictures, of course."

And with that last statement, Doug had pulled Nancy into his arms and kissed her thoroughly despite her half-hearted attempts at stalling him in case any students walked in on them.

As he walked out her classroom door, Doug turned and said "Wear something special. I'll take you out dancing afterwards."

So now Nancy was out shopping trying to find "something special." Should it be classy? Soft and feminine? Bold and daring?

"Mom?"

"What?"

"You're doing it again."

"I am? Sorry." Nancy had once again drifted off into her thoughts instead of looking at the selection of dresses that Kate and Christy had picked out for her to try.

"I really think you should wear this one, Mom." Christy was holding out a deceptively simply dress of a soft draping material – which the price tag announced cost around two weeks pay. Nancy had never paid that much for a dress in her whole life.

"I agree, Mom. It's perfect."

And with that, Nancy took the dress and tried it on. Now standing in front of the mirrored panels that showed her from several different angles, Nancy understood why the dress cost so much.

It pulled in here, tucked up there, and presented her body splendidly. The soft peach color made her skin look creamy and her eyes a clear green.

"Yep. This is it." Before she could talk herself out of it, Nancy changed back into her everyday clothes, took the dress to the cashier and put it on her credit card.

"Now, underwear." Kate was again in charge of the shopping expedition. Sincerely, if anyone ever needed someone to take over a small country single-handedly, Nancy knew that Kate was the one to do it.

"Yeah, and not old-lady underwear, either." Christy had her own opinions, too.

"Okay, but you're NOT getting me into a thong. It would be like having a perpetual wedgie." Nancy and the girls giggled about that all the way to the lingerie store.

"Besides, it isn't like he's going to see my underwear or anything." Nancy tried to keep her voice neutral.

Kate and Christy just exchanged glances behind their mom's back. Kate winked and Christy smirked.

When they finally made their purchases about forty minutes later, Nancy was bemused by the fact that she'd just spent over $200.00 on underwear that didn't amount to over eight square inches total. And who would have thought that a thong DIDN'T feel like a perpetual wedgie. In fact, her new undergarments made her feel attractive and desirable.

Now for the shoes. Something sexy, but not too come-hither. For Pete's sake, she was a mom!

They discovered that the local department store had the absolutely best shoe department anywhere! And not only was the selection extensive, but Nancy and her girls were served coffee in small demitasse cups with tiny finger pastries while the salesman brought out pair after pair of shoes for them to try.

Nancy, Kate and Christy all bought new shoes, and Nancy was especially surprised that her high heels didn't hurt her feet! Just goes to show what a pair of very expensive shoes feels like. It's sure different than a pair of tennies!

****

"If Madam would just allow me to add a few subtle highlights framing her face, she would be amazed at how much younger she would look." It had been years since Nancy had heard herself referred to in the third person while being directly addressed. And that had been in college – in a very bad play.

"Madam likes her color the way it is." Nancy tried to keep a straight face.

"Oh, come on, Mom! Try it! The worst that will happen is that you don't like it and you can get your hair dyed back to your regular color." Both Kate and Christy were determined that their mom see herself as beautiful as they both saw her.

Nancy watched "Mr. Tomas" shudder slightly at that and took pity on him.

"Alright, Mr. Tomas, you talked me into it."

And those were Nancy's final words of control for the afternoon. She was whisked off by "the shampoo girl" who did the most delightfully relaxing job of shampooing and massaging her head. She didn't want it to end, it felt so good.

Then while sitting at Mr. Tomas' regal station, Nancy found that her hair was no longer her own. Mr. Tomas had several of his salon personnel crowded around the chair while he proceeded to hold forth on the correct way to make a "woman of a certain age" look more beautiful. After unsuccessfully trying to keep up with what he was saying (fringe, shading, luminosity, depth, and angle) Nancy's thoughts drifted. She thought back to Doug's kisses. And the way he'd looked at her. And the way her heart hammered into overtime whenever he touched her. Doug knew instinctively how to touch her. And she loved the fact that he loved the back of her neck. He'd discovered that right away! Nancy sighed contentedly.

"And see? She is looking younger already! It makes her face glow." Mr. Tomas announced to his disciples who all made agreeable noises. *And my toes curl*, Nancy added to herself.

The truth was, when Mr. Tomas was done, Nancy love the way her hair looked! It looked natural, only better. And Mr. Tomas was right. The highlights were very subtle and absolutely perfect. Nancy had no qualms about paying what he charged.

CHAPTER 19

On Wednesday when Nancy got home from school with the girls she opened their front door to a flood.

"Oh, no!! There's water everywhere! What happened?" Nancy stepped into the foyer and could see water covering the floor in the kitchen and had the gruesome suspicion that the carpet in the living room and hallway were soaked.

Kate and Christy checked out the rest of the house and found that the flood had contained itself to the kitchen, foyer, living room, hallway and guest bathroom where it had all started.

The water was pouring out from the cabinet under the sink and when Nancy opened the doors, she found that the hot water pipe had corroded through. The water had been running so long that they'd drained all hot water and it was now running at lukewarm temperature.

"Okay! Who knows where the water shut-off valve is?"

Christy already had Jackson on the phone. "Yeah, babe. The pipe has a hole in it about the size of a quarter. Uh-huh. Uh-huh. Okay. Love you too." She hung up. "Jackson says to put silicone tape around it."

At that announcement, Nancy and Kate just stared at Christy. She could have been speaking Greek for all that they understood.

"Silicone tape? What's that?" Kate had already started down the hall to get Nancy's toolbox from the garage. Nancy grabbed towels off the towel bars and threw them onto the floor of the cabinet hoping they would absorb some of the water. She was starting to panic.

Just then she heard Kate's voice coming down the hall "In here! You showed up with perfect timing!"

Nancy was hoping Kate had miraculously found a plumber, but knew that would have been wishful thinking. However, she was appalled to find it was Jonathon! He walked carefully into the rapidly shrinking bathroom and put his hands on his hips. Hips wearing pink and yellow spandex that had been sitting on a bicycle seat. He looked absurd. And the half-helmet and slender sunglasses didn't help.

"Well, what did you do now?" Did those *have* to be the first words out of his mouth? Well, of course they did.

"The pipe busted while we were at school."

"That's because you moved the girls into this old dump."

Nancy thought of several retorts only to bite them back. No sense getting into an argument that she knew from historical fact she could never win.

"Are you able to help us shut off the water? I don't know where the shut off valve is."

"It's where it is for every house in Orange."

Okay. Are we going to have to go through twenty questions?

Just then there was a loud knock on the open front door.

"Nancy? You and the kids here?" Doug's voice sounded wonderful!

"We're in here, Doug!" Christy yelled down the hallway. Nancy was unable to miss the look of disapproval sent at Christy by Jonathon.

"Wow! Let me get the shut-off valve." And with that Doug was out the front door and out to the sidewalk where he opened the cement cover plate that was over the water meter, reached inside and turned something. The water under the sink slowed to a trickle and then stopped completely.

When he reappeared in the bathroom, Nancy gave him a dry towel and a beaming smile.

"Thank you! I didn't know what I was going to do." Nancy and the girls were all smiling. Jonathon's face held a look of bewilderment.

Doug glanced at Jonathon. "He would have just turned off the valve." Doug's voice didn't even hold an ounce of emotion. It was a stated fact. As though everyone just knew that Jonathon was on his way out to the meter to handle the flood, and Doug just happened to meet him.

"Well, come on, everybody. I'll make some coffee." Nancy had to squeeze between Doug and Jonathon to get out the door. As she moved past the men, Doug reached out and squeezed her shoulder with one hand. To everyone else it was a touch of human compassion. To Nancy it was a promise of things to come.

Since her back was to everyone following her down the hall, Nancy had no idea of the looks and unspoken communication that occurred between the four of them. But believe you me, there was a whole conflagration of conversation happening on a silent level.

Doug was the first to speak out loud as he entered the kitchen. "Do you have a shop vac? I'll get started on mopping up the water."

Nancy was very happy to be able to answer in the affirmative. When the divorce had first happened and she and the girls had moved out, she'd gone to the local Home Depot and purchased tools and equipment that she thought she'd need, since Jonathon had claimed everything in the garage as his.

She purchased not only a shop vac, but also a complete tool kit, extension ladder, step ladder, wheelbarrow, assorted garden tools, a Black and Decker drill with accessories (although she knew that wasn't the word the guy at Home Depot had used) and a great circular saw that she had no idea when or if she'd ever put to use. When she'd purchased the latter, she'd entertained a small fantasy of using it on Jonathon, but quickly pushed that thought to the back of her mind. Besides it would have ruined the saw.

Christy was already out the door to the garage to retrieve the requested vac.

There was an awkward silence from everyone as Jonathon moved further into the kitchen. The shoes he was wearing (he would have used the word "gear") were oddly shaped and he walked as though he was carefully stepping on hot coals. While everyone watched in fascination, he made his way over to the kitchen table, pulled out one of the dark cherry wood chairs and sat down. When his butt hit the seat the spell was broken and everyone else except Nancy started to move again.

As Doug walked past her heading for the table, his hand touched the small of her back. It was a fleeting touch, but Nancy felt branded! Gawd he could set off sparks in her!

She finished preparing the coffee maker with filter, grounds and bottled water and pushed the button to start it. Then she walked over to the table and sat next to Doug. He removed his hat and set it on the sideboard. Then he ran his hand through his hair.

Nancy looked at Jonathon and watched as he removed his helmet and reaching over, set it also on the sideboard. He ran his hand over his head. No hair, just head.

Kate couldn't help herself. "Dad! When did you shave your head?"

"Do you like it? It feels much better and everyone else seems to like it." Jonathon smiled at Kate for confirmation.

"Wow! It's sure different!" was what Kate finally managed to say.

Nancy could only stare and wonder how she had EVER found this man attractive.

Christy bustled back in the door with the new vac. "Where should I start, Mom?" Looking up, she spotted her dad's bald head. "Geez Louise, Dad! What happened?"

When Jonathon started to frown at Christy, Nancy jumped in with, "Let's get the kitchen floor with a quick sweep, then tackle the carpets. Thank goodness, it's a warm day today. Kate, could you help me open all the windows for ventilation?

Doug got up from the table "Here, I'll turn on the house fan to get the circulation going."

Nancy smiled at him and thought he could get her circulation going any time he wanted!

Two minutes later Nancy, Doug and Kate returned to the kitchen just as the coffee maker beeped that it was finished. Christy was now attacking the carpet in the hallway.

Nancy got out mugs, sugar and cream and placed them on the table. She poured the coffee and sat back down next to where Doug had once again sat.

"Nancy, you make the best coffee." Doug smelled his cup and then took a long draw of the black liquid. Nancy watched his lips touch the cup rim. He looked over the cup at her and winked. Nancy beamed.

Kate had added cream to one of the cups and had taken it to Christy.

Kate took over the vacuum detail as Christy took the cup in one hand and pulled out her cell phone with the other.

"Hey, babe! Can you pick up some silicone tape before you come over? We didn't have any. Hm-hm. Hm-hm. Okay. See you soon. Love you!" And then in a softer voice, "No, I love you more." This went on for several more seconds until Kate rolled her eyes at her sister and made pretend gagging noises.

Christy got off the phone and grinned at Kate. "Don't worry, dear sister. Someday you will find a guy as great as Jackson and then all the Adams women will be happy."

"Yeah, but my guy won't do the 'fart under the arm' routine when he's bored."

"No, but he'll do something like it. And you'll think it's the greatest, most clever thing you've ever seen."

Kate laughed. "I can hardly wait!"

While back in the kitchen ...

Doug drained his coffee, retrieved his hat and stood up. "Gotta get back to work. Dinner tonight?" He held Nancy's chair when she also stood. Jonathon just sat and watched. He hadn't touched his coffee.

"I'm making meatloaf tonight. Sound good to you? I'd rather not go out. There's a lot of cleaning to do here."

"Sounds great. What time?"

"Seven o'clock?"

"I'll be here." Doug held out his right hand towards Jonathon. "Good to see you again."

At least Jonathon had the presence of mind to return the handshake. "Yeah."

With that, Nancy walked Doug to the door. He shouted into the living room. "Kate, Christy, see you later!"

Nancy heard her daughters answer something over the sound of the shop vac starting back up.

Doug leaned down and gently touched his lips to Nancy's. "Catch YOU later." And taking her breath with him, he went out to his car, got in, and backed out of the driveway.

Nancy smiled to herself and walked back into the kitchen in order to pull a pound of hamburger out of the freezer for their dinner.

When she entered the kitchen she fell back to earth when she saw her ex sitting at her table. "Did you need to see me for something?" She was less than enthusiastic.

"How long have you been seeing him?" Jonathon's tone was disapproving. Was there any other way he spoke to her? Was it ONLY her? How did he have any friends with that attitude?

"Actually, that's none of your business." Nancy opened the freezer and pulled out a white wrapped package of meat.

"It is if he's around my girls."

Nancy placed the package on the counter and turned to Jonathon. "He's a decorated member of the police force. What disagreements could you possibly have about Doug?"

"I want my daughters safe."

"Well, you should have considered that when you refused joint custody." Nancy paused before saying what she'd been wanting to say now for a long time. "I still can't believe that if you see the girls more than one day a week, we lose some of the child support money! The girls literally have to pay to see their father."

"It's only fair. If I see them that often, they I'm paying for more food and utilities."

Nancy could only shake her head in wonderment. It never occurred to her to count the money she spent on her daughters. It's what parents did! And to be honest, there was no way that the money Jonathon spent on child support even came close to covering the girls' expenses. It certainly helped, but the amount was NOT the sole support for the girls.

Nancy drew in a cleansing breath and slowly released it. "What do you want, Jonathon?" She refused to let him get to her anymore.

"Oh. I was cycling past and wanted to show Kate and Christy my new bike. I thought they'd like to see it."

Could he be any denser? New bike? The reason the child support check was always late was because 'he didn't have the money.' But he could afford a new toy. Of course.

"Then I think you should show it to them."

With that statement, Nancy turned her attention to preparing dinner.

Jonathon hobbled out of the kitchen without even a 'thank you for the coffee' and called for the girls. Nancy could hear their voices, but not what they were saying. She then saw Jonathon carefully walk out the door, get on his bike and ride off.

Okay, curiosity got the better of her and Nancy went into the living room. The girls had just taken the tub of extracted water down the hall and dumped it down the toilet. They were reattaching the tub to the vac.

"Didn't you want to see your dad's new bike?"

"Oh, we'll see it later, Mom. Right now we've only got about three more hours of daylight and we want to get the carpet as dry as possible before dark."

Oh. That makes perfectly good sense. Nancy returned to the kitchen and missed the look that passed between her daughters.

"I'm surprised that Mom never killed him before. Has Dad always been this unconnected with reality?" Christy was much harsher in her condemnation of Jonathon than Kate was.

"I don't think he means to be this uptight. He just doesn't get it. If he thought that he was actually harming us, he'd be really upset." Kate probably had the best perspective on Jonathon's behavior than anyone else in the family did.

....

A couple of hours later, Nancy was happy to see Doug pull up in his truck. She watched in wonder as he got out of the cab, moved to the back of the truck bed and grabbed a portable fan in each hand. Of course! More air flow onto the carpet.

Jackson had shown up earlier and fixed the hole in the pipe. After he turned the water back on, he admonished Nancy to contact the landlord so that he could get a plumber out to the house. Nancy reluctantly made the phone call. Thank goodness, Jackson was still at the house when the landlord showed up. Mr. Volk made her and the girls uncomfortable, so it felt much better to have another male right there.

After trying to explain to Nancy that the situation didn't require a plumber, Mr. Volk finally agreed to call one when Jackson used 'handyman-speak' and convinced the landlord that he didn't want the whole house's plumbing to burst and destroy the house's 'structural integrity.'

Nancy gave Jackson a hug after Mr. Volk had left and she could tell that Jackson was proud of the way he'd helped. Christy beamed.

Since the front door was propped open for the airflow, Doug came directly into the living room and set up the fans to blow at angles across the carpet.

When he'd finished with that task, he went into the kitchen where Nancy was checking on the meatloaf in the oven. She'd just straightened and pulled off the hot mitts when Doug's arms snaked around her from behind and drew her into his embrace. They stood there for a while with Nancy leaning her head back onto his chest and Doug leaning his cheek against the top of her hair. She could feel the muscles in his forearms where her hands rested. Strong forearms.

They stood that way for several minutes, then Doug gave her a quick kiss and went to help the girls with the carpet. Nancy finished dinner, humming to herself.

When everyone finally sat down, they were famished and the meal was consumed in a satisfied silence.

When Nancy went to bed that night, she felt herself blush, again remembering what Doug had whispered in her ear after kissing her until she thought she'd never be able to breathe again. He was so good for her.

CHAPTER 20

The rest of that week was magical. Nancy saw Doug everyday when he'd stop by her classroom at the end of the school day and they'd make plans for dinner that night. Several times he just had dinner at her house with her and the kids. Nancy was even thinking of inviting him for Thanksgiving dinner, but she'd check with the kids first.

Doug seemed to get along with her kids and they seemed to really like him.

One of Nancy's favorite evenings happened after a macaroni and cheese dinner; the kids took off around 7:00 pm for a concert in which one of Jackson's friends was playing. That meant that Nancy and Doug had the house to themselves. And boy! Did they put it to good use!

They talked. And talked. And were still talking at 11:00 pm when the kids got home. In fact they hadn't moved from their chairs at the dining table and the dinner dishes still hadn't been touched.

"So what did you guys do while we were gone, anyway?" Christy was standing in the kitchen with her hands on her hips looking at the dinner mess.

Nancy and Doug looked at each other, smiled and then looked at the kids.

"We, ah, talked." Doug sounded more baffled than guilty, although he knew that the kids suspected hanky-panky.

"Talked." Jackson wasn't buying it.

"Yep. Just talked." Nancy got up from the table, grabbed Doug's hand as she went past his chair and pulled him into the foyer next to the front door.

"We left the dishes for you guys." Nancy patted Christy's arm as she passed her.

When they were out of sight of the kids, she wrapped her arms around Doug's waist and laid her head on his chest.

"I really can't believe we just talked." Running his hand up and down Nancy's back, Doug still sounded bemused. "We had enough time to do anything we wanted. But we talked." He gathered Nancy tighter against him and rested his cheek on top of her head.

"I liked it." Nancy's voice was muffled against Doug's chest.

"Me, too." Doug's voice was muffled against Nancy's hair.

"This feels so good. Can we just stay this way forever?" Nancy pulled away just enough to lift her face to Doug's.

"Sounds good to me, Sweetheart." Doug actually did a fairly good job of mimicking Bogart.

"I suppose it's time for you to go, isn't it?" Nancy just gazed into Doug's eyes.

"Yes. It is." He didn't move.

"Okay." She didn't move either.

Finally Doug leaned down and kissed Nancy softly on the lips.

"I love you." he breathed.

Nancy's smile was radiant. "I love you, too."

Doug smiled into Nancy's eyes. "I've got to be honest though. I thought I'd be saying that to you the first time we made love. And here I'm saying it and I haven't even gotten to second base yet."

Nancy just about choked on her laughter. "Second base? I haven't heard that term in years! Well here, Officer. Just so your evening wasn't a complete waste." Nancy took Doug's left hand and after checking that none of the kids were within sight or sound distance, she put Doug's hand up under her shirt and covered her right breast with it.

Doug's breath caught in his throat and his eyes darkened. Smiling, he pulled Nancy closer with his right arm and while kissing her, gently moved his thumb over the peak of her breast. He felt her breath hitch and he did it again -- and again.

Nancy finally pulled back for air.

She hadn't felt this excited since her first high school necking session. "Okay. You can now officially tell the guys that you made it to second base."

"I never tell the guys. This is way too personal. Besides you mean too much to me for me to be indiscrete. Remember, I love you."

With that final statement, Doug released Nancy and opened the front door.

He leaned back to her and gave her one last thorough kiss.

"Catch you later."

Little did Nancy know that it would be over six weeks before she saw Doug again.

PAT ADEFF

CHAPTER 21

"Where is he?" Doug demanded to know when he got to the station.

"Downstairs in a holding cell."

Doug took the stairs two at a time down to the two holding cells that the OPD had in their basement.

Stretched out on the concrete shelf in one of the cells was his son, Andy, snoring and drooling.

"Let me in there." Doug growled at the officer on duty.

"No way, Saunders. He's asked for his attorney and we can't do anything until the guy gets here. You know the rules."

"He's my son, damn it!" Doug didn't know if he wanted to throttle the kid or smother him in a hug.

When he'd gotten the call right after he'd left Nancy's house, Doug'd been told that Andy had been involved with a hit and run. Now seeing him passed out in the tank, he was torn between being grateful that Andy hadn't been injured, and furious that he'd been drinking and driving. The kid he'd hit was going to be fine. It was one of Andy's buddies, Chad, with whom he'd been out drinking. According to witnesses, Andy had gunned the car, goofing around. Chad had stupidly jumped in front of the car and suddenly the car had gone into gear and hit Chad. Luckily for Chad he'd also been drunk and just rolled off the car.

It got tricky when Andy had then taken off out of the parking lot. The witnesses had called paramedics and Chad was taken to the hospital for observation and a couple of stitches on his elbow from where he'd hit the ground.

The call had gone out and Andy had been apprehended within just a couple of minutes by Bill Winston, who'd brought him straight to the OPD on Struck Street.

Now Andy was sleeping it off while Doug wanted to tear the kid's head off.

Andy rolled over and through blurry eyes spotted Doug. "Oh, hey, there Officer. Whattare you doin' here?" Andy's eyes got wider as he looked around the cell. "Oops! I guess I'm in trouble."

"Trouble isn't even the beginning of what you're going to go through." Doug had both of his hands clasped around two of the bars and could smell the alcohol from where he was standing.

"Did we get a blood-alcohol level yet?"

"It's not back from the lab yet, Doug," Bill Winston said as he entered the room. "Take your break, Bob. I'll watch for now."

"Thanks, Bill. I'll be back in fifteen." Bob went up the stairs to the break room.

"Let me in there," Doug said to Bill.

"Nope. No way." Bill put a hand on Doug's shoulder.

"Thatsa spirit, Officer," Andy tried to focus on Bill. "Don't lettem get me."

"I'll get you myself, you little punk, if you don't shut your mouth." Bill knew exactly how angry Doug was and also knew that right now he was the only thing keeping Andy from getting his lights punched out.

Just then, they heard a female voice coming down the stairs. "Swear to God, you little good-for-nothing. You better have a good reason for what you've done." Andy's mom flew from the stairwell into the room, where she came up short and stopped, looking first at Doug and then at Bill and finally at Andy in the tank.

"What the hell were you thinking, Andy?" Sue rushed over to the bars. "Chad could have been killed!"

"Whadaya talkin about, Mom? Where's Chad?" Andy looked puzzled.

"Chad's in the hospital, you idiot! You hit him with your car. He had to have stitches."

Doug had stepped back from the cell and watched this mother-son exchange through troubled eyes. If only he'd been there from the beginning, maybe this wouldn't be happening.

Andy had started to cry, soft sobs between hiccups.

"I hit Chad? But he's my friend."

"Bob said an attorney was on the way. Do you know which one?" Doug questioned Sue.

"Bradley Harris, I think. Andy's gonna need the best criminal defense attorney I can afford."

"WE can afford. I'll help with the cost." Doug put a hand on Sue's shoulder. "Maybe if I'd been there for him sooner, he wouldn't be here right now."

Sue shrugged his hand off and said, "Doug, I never allowed you near him. This isn't your problem."

"Yes it is. He's my son, too, whether I helped raise him or not.

Please let me help now. I want to."

Sue considered Doug's request and said she'd think about it.

Andy had fallen back on the concrete shelf and was amazingly asleep again.

"Let him sleep it off Doug. Come back at the end of shift. Maybe he'll be more coherent then." Bill hated seeing Doug like this. He knew his friend was blaming himself for Andy's current condition.

Doug looked at Sue, who was looking at Andy. "Yeah. I think I'll go home. Sue, call me tomorrow. I really want to help." Doug turned away and went up the stairs.

After a minute, Sue turned to Bill. "How's Doug doing? He looks good."

"He's doing fine."

Sue stood there with her arms crossed in front of her, gazing at her son. "I heard Doug's got a new girlfriend."

Boy, word sure travels fast in the department.

As Sue sat down on one of the hard plastic chairs outside the cell, Bill thought he heard her say something like, "Lucky lady. Didn't know what I had."

Bill couldn't have agreed more.

As Doug came out of the top of the stairwell, he almost ran into the sergeant, who seemed to be waiting for him.

"More trouble with Andy? You know, Doug, it's been proven that kids from broken homes have a harder time with the law." The smirk on the sergeant's mouth was begging for a fist.

With extreme self-control, Doug was able to walk past the jerk without killing him. Doug kept walking to the exit door without acknowledging what the sergeant had said. Just as his hand touched the door handle, he heard a snort from the sergeant.

"About time you decided to get involved with your son."

Doug kept walking. Although it would have felt great to squash the guy like a bug, he had bigger problems to attend to. He'd save the sergeant for a day he was bored with nothing better to do.

....

The next morning, Nancy frowned as she placed the phone receiver back into its cradle.

"Was that Doug, Mom?" Kate asked before Christy had the chance to. They were sitting at the dining room table pouring over a bridal magazine making plans for Christy and Jackson's wedding, although Nancy hoped it wasn't going to happen for at least another year.

"Yes. Doug's son has been arrested for hit and run while under the influence." Nancy slowly shook her head back and forth then looked at her girls. "Thank you so much for not being like that."

Both girls got up and moved over to Nancy and the three of them stood with their arms around each other for several moments.

"Oh, YES! Group hug!" Jackson called out as he bounded into the kitchen. He ran over and wrapped his arms mostly around Christy while everyone laughed.

"Thank you, Jackson. I needed that." Nancy wiped her eyes and smiled at him.

"I do what I can, Momma A." Jackson was giving Nancy his patented "I own the world" grin.

"I imagine Doug could use someone like you right about now," Nancy said thoughtfully.

"Is he coming over here tonight?" Kate asked.

"No. He said he'd get back to me. That for now, Bill and Patty's ceremony has been postponed." Nancy added to herself, I sure hope I hear from him sooner rather than later.

It was actually six weeks later. Six of the longest weeks in Nancy's life.

A few days later after she'd gotten home from work, Jonathon showed up again at their doorstep. Nancy couldn't believe it. She'd seen her ex more in the past 30 days than she had the entire first two years after the divorce.

She bit back a sigh and said "I need to run over to the school. I left something there." Jonathon just stood there, not acknowledging her, nor giving any indication of what he wanted. Nancy looked pointedly at the papers in his hand.

"Can I just wait here until you get back? We need to both sign this. It's an old addendum for some taxes that our accountant missed."

Nancy almost rolled her eyes. "Of course. Help yourself to coffee if you want. I should only be gone about 10 minutes."

With that, she grabbed her purse and keys and headed out for the folder of papers she'd left on her desk.

Since he had the house to himself, Jonathon took his time looking around at what she'd done with the place. Lots of color, which he found garish. He frowned when he realized that none of the pictures in the hallway included him. They were all pictures of Nancy and the girls with various friends.

Jonathon hesitated for a moment when the phone rang. He knew he should probably let the call go to voicemail, but something had him reaching for the receiver. "Hello?"

Doug hesitated for a moment when he hear Jonathon's voice answering Nancy's phone. What was he doing there?

"Hey. It's Doug Saunders. Is Nancy there?"

Jonathon smiled to himself. "No. She just stepped out for a minute. Could I take a message? I'll be here when she gets back."

Well, what the hell was that supposed to mean? Doug didn't like the tone of Jonathon's voice. Sort of like he was one-upping him in some way.

"Yeah, sure. She can call at her convenience. She has the number." Doug tried to sound calm, when he really wanted to reach through the phone line and wipe the smirk he could hear from Jonathon's face.

"Not a problem, Doug. Although I don't think she'll have time to call you before tomorrow, if you know what I mean. Hope you don't mind." Jonathon was having entirely too much fun with the conversation, and kept loading his words with innuendo of some sort.

Doug pulled the phone away from his ear and snarled at it. Gathering his patience, he reluctantly thanked Jonathon and hung up. What the ...? Is Nancy getting back together with Jonathon? That didn't make any sense. Doug figured he'd wait to talk to her when she called him back.

What Doug didn't know, was that Jonathon had no intention of letting Nancy know he'd called. In fact, Jonathon actually forgot about the call when Nancy returned and they spent the next 20 minutes sorting out who owed what on the missed taxes.

Nancy went to bed that night, wishing that she'd hear from Doug. She knew he was busy with Andy, but she really missed him.

The next evening, when Doug still hadn't heard from Nancy, he started to imagine the worst. It didn't help when he drove past her house and saw Jonathon's car was in the driveway. If he'd only known that Jonathon was only there for the 10 minutes it had taken him to drop off the revised tax forms and get Nancy's signature.

The next Monday, Nancy saw a picture in the Orange Daily News of Andy being escorted into the courthouse with his attorney, Bradley Harris in front, and Doug and Sue on either side of Andy. Doug's hand was reaching across Andy's back and was resting on Sue's shoulder. Sue was looking over at Doug. The black and white print was grainy, but vivid. Sue was looking at Doug with love in her eyes.

Nancy's stomach dropped when she wondered if Sue was the reason that Doug hadn't called. She wondered if Doug was starting to feel sorry he'd gone out with Nancy. She wondered if he'd ever call.

Nancy tried to be philosophical about Doug's lack of communication. No use borrowing trouble as her grandpa used to say. She'd just have to wait and see. She'd left one message at the station for him but hadn't heard back. She knew he'd call if he wanted to.

She hoped he wanted to.

Doug was now on the night shift, which left his days open so he could spend time with his son. The judge showed compassion and Andy went immediately into a rehab program. With both his mom and dad paying attention to him, he was calming down and making some changes in the way he viewed his life. Andy knew that he would have to make some rather large changes, and pretty fast, or he'd be dead before he hit 30.

Sue had been being especially nice to Doug and their friendship was almost back to where it had been when they'd been partners on the force. Doug could tell that Sue wanted more, but he wasn't interested in her that way. It still made Doug mentally flinch a little to remember one of the incidents with Sue after a day in court…

He'd driven Sue home after they'd spent several hours with Andy at the rehab center after court that day. Andy was having a hard time adjusting to the restrictions that were mandatory at the center and today had been an especially difficult one. It didn't help that he was still having to get used to no alcohol, especially when Andy had the habit of drinking when he was stressed. When Sue had moved to give him a hug before she and Doug left, Andy had been surly which had upset Sue even more.

Pulling into Sue's driveway, Doug shifted the car into park but didn't turn off the engine. Sue turned to Doug and asked him tearfully if he'd come in, just to check the house for her.

Doug reluctantly agreed, turned off the engine and stepped out of the car. What he really wanted to do was go home, take a shower and call Nancy. They walked up to the front door and Sue dug around in her purse while Doug shifted from foot to foot. She finally got the front door unlocked, reached inside and flipped on the lights. Doug stepped into the house and went from room to room, checking to ensure that the windows were still secured and everything was okay.

He came down the hall to the kitchen where he heard Sue rummaging around. Doug stepped into the kitchen and Sue turned from the counter and handed him an opened beer bottle. Doug turned and set it on the table without drinking from it. Sue took a large drink from her bottle.

"Everything's secure, so I'll be going now." Doug turned to walk down the hall.

"Wait, Doug." Sue moved towards him. "I wanted to thank you for everything you've done for us – for Andy and me. And also to apologize for keeping you from your son all these years. You didn't deserve that."

Sue set her beer bottle down on the counter and moved closer to

Doug. She reached out to him. Doug stepped back.

Sue looked beseechingly at him. "It's just a hug. I could really use one right now." Her eyes brimmed with tears.

Doug felt like a jerk for having suspected her motives and stepping towards her, took her into his embrace for a hug. Sue clung to him while she cried. He felt a jumble of emotions that threatened to swamp him. Guilt, pity, sorrow, and anger at himself.

They stood that way for quite a while until Sue's sobs diminished – Sue clinging to Doug and Doug holding her gently and rubbing her back in a "there-there" motion. Finally she pulled back and wiped her eyes on her sleeve. Doug looked around the kitchen and found the paper towels. Pulling one off the roll, he handed it to her with a small smile. "I know it's not soft, but it's better than a sleeve."

Sue gave a small hiccup and smiled at Doug as she took the offered paper towel. "You know, Doug. I was really stupid to let you go."

"Sue, we never were really together. It was a one-time aberration. Nothing more." Doug tried to keep his voice even, but compassionate.

"How can you say that? We have a son together." Sue looked hurt. She grabbed her beer and drained it.

"Come on, Sue. You and I both know *that* won't handle anything." Doug gestured towards now empty beer bottle.

"Do not lecture me, Doug. I don't need the grief right now."

"Sue, you're right. I'm sorry. Look, we both don't need the grief right now."

They stood there awkwardly in the kitchen for several heartbeats.

"Doug?"

"Hm-m-m?"

"Do you … is there any chance … Damn! This is hard to say." Sue rubbed her forehead with the back of her wrist.

Doug was starting to feel really uneasy. "Then don't say it, Sue."

"**No**. No. I have to. Is there any chance you could eventually feel anything for me again?" Sue was looking at him with such longing.

Doug reached out and put his hands on her shoulders. "Sue, I just can't."

"Is there someone else?"

At the thought of Nancy and the way he'd ignored her the past few weeks, Doug cringed inwardly.

"I hope so. I hope I haven't blown it. But, Sue, the truth is that even if there wasn't someone else, there wouldn't be a 'you and me' either."

"Yeah, you're right. I know that. I just had to ask." Sue was starting to look embarrassed.

"Don't be upset. You're a great gal. And if there wasn't anyone else, it would be a smart move on my part to be with you. After all, you are the mother of my son." Doug hoped that would make Sue feel better.

"Saunders, you are a lousy liar. You were even back when we were partners. But, I've always admired your class." Sue looked back to being herself.

"Yeah. Well, your class made up for the both of us."

"Goodnight Doug."

"Goodnight Sue."

"Hey, Doug."

"Yeah?"

"Don't worry. I won't come on to you again."

Doug reached out and gave Sue a brotherly hug. "You're the best."

"Catch ya later." Sue smiled and closed the front door behind him.

Doug went home. He took a shower and tried really hard to get up the courage to call Nancy. You know, for being a cop, there were times he sure could be chickenshit.

....

For the next several weeks, all of his thoughts were with a divorced mom of two, renting a house just a few blocks away from the station.

Late at night, Doug would drive his unit past Nancy's house and wish that he could just pull into her driveway, go inside and have a cup of coffee with her. He wanted so badly to tell her he was sorry that he was such a screw up as a dad, and that he was also sorry he'd stopped calling her. Once he realized that a week had passed and he hadn't seen Nancy or spoken with her, he started to feel guilty, which made it harder for him to just pick up the phone and call her.

After the picture came out in the paper, Doug was sure that Nancy would think the worst and would want nothing more to do with him. She didn't need to get involved with a cop! She had a nice life, great kids and a wonderful job. He'd just mess it up for her. And he still wasn't sure that she and Jonathon weren't getting back together.

One night Doug actually pulled into her driveway and turned off the engine, planning to go to her and explain everything, but it was 1:00 in the morning and no lights were on. He sat there willing Nancy to turn on her bedroom light, or go into the kitchen and see him sitting out there waiting for her, and come out to him like she had before. But no lights came on, and no Nancy came to him.

Doug reluctantly started up the engine and pulled slowly down the block, missing the light that came on in Nancy's kitchen when she looked out to see who had pulled into her driveway.

She'd been hoping it was Doug, but no one was there.

Foolish woman, Nancy chided herself and doubts crept further in. Why in the world would someone like Doug want someone like her? Nancy walked slowly back to bed feeling very tired and very old.

PAT ADEFF

CHAPTER 22

"Okay, thanks guys! Great job!" Nancy stood and smiled at the drama students as they exited the theatre.

"Bye!" "Hope I get the part!" "When do we find out?" The students spoke excitedly as they left. Nancy just smiled and waved at them all. She gathered the audition sheets and the copies of the script they'd used for the try-outs. Everyone knew that she'd make the casting decisions over the upcoming four-day Thanksgiving weekend.

Auditions were always exciting and way too much work; but worth it all when it finally came to opening night. And surprise of surprises, for once she had the principal's son in attendance. Nancy had always felt that Russell had the makings of an excellent actor; he'd just never really seemed to want to try before. Now he'd auditioned for the male lead and was actually in the running for getting the part! Nancy hoped that the other boys wouldn't feel that she was playing favorites if she cast Russell for the role. The politics involved with casting a school play were sometimes more than she wanted to deal with.

And speaking of dealing with. What was she going to do with all her emotions regarding Doug? She hadn't heard from him in weeks. Her kids were still trying to get her to call the station again, but she didn't want to look like she was chasing him.

This was worse than high school! Nancy still blushed when she remembered how inane she felt when she saw Doug drive past her house last weekend. She chastised herself for still feeling hurt that he hadn't stopped, but she couldn't make the yearning go away. And for the life of her, she couldn't figure out what Doug was thinking.

Well, as Kate said, "Ask him!"

Nancy wished that she could be as level headed as her older daughter seemed to be when it came to dealing with men. Kate must have gotten that analytical ability from Jonathon. It sure hadn't come from Nancy. Nancy was more of the "tell me you love me and I'm yours forever" type of gal.

Which brought her thoughts back full circle to Doug. He'd said that he loved her. He had been tender, sweet, sexy, warm and attentive. He'd said the words and then he'd disappeared. Nancy didn't know what to think about that. She loved him so much. She'd been walking across the stage with her papers in her arms and stopped dead in her tracks with the realization. She really loved Doug. She hadn't actually thought that she'd ever feel this way again. She had prepared herself for being single the rest of her life. Now, this wonderful, virile man had entered her life and had made her feel young and beautiful again. And now she had a broken heart. Love hurts! Weren't there just about a million songs about heartbreak? Of course there were, and she'd heard every single one of them over the past few weeks. It seemed like no matter which radio station she tuned in, there had been some song that exactly matched her mood. She'd given up listening to the radio, just so she could spare herself the pain. But then she went online and bought Dolly Parton's *I Will Always Love You*. Sigh. What a masochist.

"Ms. Adams?"

Nancy turned to see who had called to her from the back of the auditorium. It was Principal Newman's son. Russell walked down the audience aisle towards her as she crossed to the front of the stage to meet him.

"Hi, Russell. What can I do for you?" Nancy shifted the stack of papers from one arm to the other. She really hoped he wasn't going to ask her about who she was going to cast in the lead.

"Ms. Adams, I just wanted to let you know that I'm willing to take any part you want to give me. I'd be lying if I said I didn't want the lead, but I understand how much trouble it might cause to have the principal's son get that part." Russell reached up to take the papers from Nancy, as she started to sit on the apron of the stage in order to jump down into the audience section.

"Thank you, Russell. Your insight is right on the money. I was just thinking about that situation and how I should handle it." Nancy took the papers back from him and they started to walk out into the lobby.

"Actually my mom made me come find you." Russell smiled. "She didn't want you to feel any pressure from either her or me. But I do agree with her. And I would be very happy to take any role you gave me." Russell looked and sounded very sincere, but there was an underlying feeling that Nancy wasn't able to pin yet.

"So! Are you casting Carol for any specific part?" Russell had tried so hard to appear casual with his question that it took all Nancy's self-restraint not to grin at his very apparent interest in the young brunette who'd also auditioned that afternoon.

Nancy tried but couldn't resist. "Is Carol the reason you tried out for this show, Russell? It would help me make my decision on the casting if I knew whether you really wanted the part, or if you'd be just as happy being part of the crew."

Russell shoved his hands into the front pockets of his jeans and looked at the floor. By now they'd reached the front doors. Nancy stopped walking and turned to look at Russell. He turned towards her but still kept his eyes on the floor with such intentness that he reminded Nancy of her girls when they had been little and searching for candy and colored eggs on Easter mornings at home.

"Russell, you know that anything you tell me stays with me." If he only knew how much Nancy totally understood the pain that he was going through right now.

"Ms. Adams, if you cast Carol but can't cast me in the lead, at least don't cast Frankie opposite her. Please?" At that last word, Russell looked up from the floor and Nancy could see just how strongly he felt about what he'd just said. Nancy thought you couldn't pay her enough money to be seventeen again. Emotions ran way too strong, and feelings were felt way too deeply.

Yeah, like she wasn't in a similar boat right now herself.

"Russell. I understand completely, and I promise that I won't cast Frankie opposite Carol. But you do remember that acting is just that – acting. It's called acting because the actors pretend their emotions on stage." Nancy had never taught Method Acting because she'd always felt that anyone could make themselves look sad by thinking about something awful in their past. But it took real acting to make the audience think you were sad on stage, when really you were having the time of your life! She'd followed the lives of too many actors who'd studied Method Acting and had watched their personal lives disintegrate, while truthfully their craft hadn't improved that much.

Russell blew out a breath and grinned. "Thanks, Ms. A. You're the best!" With that he bounded out into the sunshine. Nancy laughed to herself. He reminded her of a Labrador puppy. All feet and ears and endless enthusiasm.

She wished her life could be handled so simply. Nancy could just picture herself walking up to Bradley Harris and saying "Bradley, please don't have Doug and Sue sit together at the courthouse." Nancy smiled and pushed open the door to the outside just as her cell phone rang.

She fumbled with the paper stack and finally pushed the talk button by the fifth ring.

"This is Nancy."

"Mom?" It was Kate, once again sounded distraught. Her voice tone set Nancy's nerves on alert, since she knew just how much it took to rattle Kate.

"Honey? What's up?" Nancy held her breath.

"Oh, Mom!" Kate wailed. "I feel so stupid! I let Robert drive when I borrowed your car this afternoon and now we were in a fender bender! I'm so sorry! It was stupid of me! I feel so bad!"

Nancy breathed a sigh of relief. "Honey? Is anyone hurt? I don't care about the car, just you." Robert was the newest boyfriend.

Kate expelled a shaky laugh. "Mom, I told Robert you'd say that, but he wouldn't believe me. We're fine. No one's hurt. Your front right fender is dented and the other lady's front bumper is messed up pretty good. Robert miscalculated and turned in front of her car when he should have waited. We're waiting for the police to show up so we can get the report for the insurance company."

"Where are you, Honey? I'll meet you there." Nancy had reached her classroom by this time and thankfully dropped the papers out of her arms onto the desk. She reached for her purse and headed out the door.

Nancy got directions from Kate and fortuitously ran into Tess who was able to drop her at the accident site on her way home from work.

When they pulled up at the curb Nancy's heart stopped beating and her breath caught in her throat. Of all the officers in the world and all the accidents. There but Doug, looking absolutely great!

Tess gave Nancy's left arm a pat and wished her good luck. Tess had watched the roller coaster ride that Nancy had been on recently and sincerely hoped that this opportunity for Nancy to speak with Doug would help.

Nancy walked over to where Doug was standing with his back to her while writing on a clipboard and listening to Kate and Robert.

"Mom!" Kate moved swiftly past Doug into Nancy's arms for a quick hug. "I am so sorry for the damage to your car and Robert and I will pay for fixing it!"

"Hon, I'm just glad you're alright." Nancy had to fight back tears because of the reminder of the motorcycle accident Christy and Jackson had been in months ago. She wiped her eyes and looked up to see Doug standing three feet in front of her.

The remainder of the world stopped while their eyes locked and they both held their breaths. Nancy's emotions were running riot inside of her. She couldn't tell what Doug was thinking and truly wished he'd say something.

Doug felt his insides twist up with the longing to take Nancy in his arms and just hold her. But he no longer felt that he had that right. God! He'd missed her so much. He was lost in her eyes.

When Doug didn't say anything, Nancy grimaced and decided that he must not feel the same way she did, so she said the first thing that came to her mind so he wouldn't feel pity for her.

"Thank you for being here, Officer Saunders. I'm glad you're the one to help Kate." Nancy congratulated herself on sounding friendly, but not anything more than that.

She was going to get through this conversation if it killed her. And truth be told, it felt like a knife was stabbing her in the heart. She missed him so much her heart hurt.

Doug exhaled and tried to hide his feeling of rejection. He'd hoped that Nancy still felt for him the way he felt for her. But it was obvious from her demeanor that what they'd shared hadn't meant as much to her as it had to him. Boy, had his misread it, or what?

"Doug. You can call me Doug, Nancy." He tried to sound normal.

Nancy saw him put on his "cop face" and wished with all her heart that she had the courage to say, *Doug, don't close me out. I love you. I miss you. I don't care what you feel for me, but I want you to know just how much you mean to me. My life has been awful these past few weeks without you. Please, let's try again.*

Instead, she said "Okay. Doug. Is there anything else you need from us?"

His gut twisted inside. "No, Nancy. I've got everything I need for the report. I can drop it by tomorrow if you want."

Please say that you want me to, Nancy. Please show me that I mean something to you.

Oh, God. He looked so incredibly good standing there! If she didn't get out of his vicinity soon, she'd make a fool of herself.

"You don't have to go to all that trouble, Doug. You can just mail it."

His jaw clenched with anger and hurt.

"Fine. That's what I'll do."

Her eyes narrowed with pain. "Fine."

And with that, Nancy walked over to her car and slipped into the driver's seat. Kate sat in front and Robert quietly took the backseat.

As Nancy drove away she glanced in the rear view mirror and saw Doug standing there watching as her car pulled away. His feet were set wide and his hands were on his hips. He looked like some warrior facing the enemy. Nancy felt her heart crack in two.

Doug watched as Nancy pulled away. It was obvious from her last statement that she sure didn't want him coming to her house. Doug wasn't aware of how long he stood there, but it was way past the time her car had disappeared from sight.

Out of sight, out of mind? No way. Doug's thoughts churned as he got back into his unit and radioed in to dispatch. It was going to be a very long time before he would be able to erase Nancy from his thoughts. Her soft skin, her green eyes, the way she looked after he'd kissed her that time, with her hair is disarray and her lips open in wonder.

She'd made him feel so needed and wanted. She'd made him feel like the world's greatest, most handsome guy. Like some sort of hero.

And now he felt like the world's biggest fool. He slammed his car into drive and then stopped and pulled his emotions together. That's all he needed right now; to do something stupid while on duty.

By the time Nancy parked in her driveway, she'd pulled herself together enough to hopefully not show any emotion to Kate. They'd dropped Robert at his house and Nancy had accepted all fifteen of

Robert's apologies and promises to pay for the car damage. Nancy had assured him that she was just glad that they hadn't been hurt. And she meant it. It was just a car.

They walked in through the front door, and Nancy put her purse on the front table.

"Honey, I think I'm going to take a nap. Are you sure you're not hurt?" Nancy smiled at Kate.

Kate folder her arms and just looked at Nancy.

"What?!" Nancy sounded to her own ears like one of her students after she'd caught them doing something they weren't supposed to be doing.

"Mom, how long are you going to keep this up?" Kate sounded ticked off at her!

"Keep what up?" Nancy couldn't believe just how lame she sounded.

"You know exactly what I'm talking about." Kate pinned Nancy with a look.

Nancy felt defensive and hurt. Why should Kate be mad at HER? She wasn't the one who'd disappear from this relationship with Doug – if that's what you could call it. He'd made it pretty clear that he was no longer interested in her.

And it hurt like hell.

"I'm tired. We'll talk later." With that, Nancy walked to her room and shut the door.

She didn't even kick off her shoes. She just fell down on the bed and curled into a ball. Slowly the tears started to run down her face onto the pillow. It was a silent cry. No sobs. No keening. Just tears that kept running.

At some point Nancy fell asleep and didn't wake up until she smelled something cooking. As she slowly sat up and mopped her face, she realized that she was really hungry! Why didn't grief make her appetite disappear? Then at least she'd have the solace of being thin while single. Oh, well.

Nancy splashed cold water on her eyes hoping to lessen their puffiness and finally ended up resorting to an old trick she'd learned decades ago from an actress she had trained with. She pulled out a witch hazel pad and dabbed it below and over her eyes. After about 3 minutes she could see a difference and felt a little better. She ran a brush through her hair and gave herself a quick inspection in the mirror. Okay, she didn't look too bad.

Nancy looked like hammered beefsteak, Kate thought when Nancy came into the kitchen. Christy and Jackson had just finished setting the table and had already been given the full rundown from Kate, so they knew to be quiet about how Nancy looked or acted.

"Perfect timing! Dinner's ready!" Kate sounded and looked normal, as did Christy and Jackson. Oh good, Nancy thought. I don't look as devastated as I feel!

It took all the acting powers that Kate, Christy and Jackson had to just get through the dinner. They'd never seen Nancy look so bad before. It was as though someone had taken away all her perpetual optimism and left her just an empty shell.

At the end of dinner, Nancy started to grab the empty plates, but Christy took them instead.

"It's okay, Mom. It's Jackson and my turn to do the dishes. Kate cooked tonight." Christy nudged Jackson in the shoulder when he didn't stand right away and they both grabbed plates, glasses and silverware and carried them to the sink.

Nancy just sat there wondering what she was supposed to do now. She didn't want to watch a movie. She didn't want to read. It was only 7:00 pm and she wasn't tired after the nap. She'd already bought everything she needed for Thanksgiving dinner.

As though reading her mind, Kate asked "Hey, Mom? Do you want to go shopping with me? I need to buy some Christmas presents and I don't want to wait until the last minute."

That sounded great! Nancy had a few items to get herself, and this would be perfect. The downtown shops didn't close until 10:00 pm during the holidays, so they had a couple of hours.

"Sure, honey. Let me get my jacket." Nancy left the kitchen and missed the weighted looks that her kids gave to each other.

"We've got to do something about this!" Jackson said. "This is killing her!" He rinsed and handed the plates to Christy while she loaded them into the dishwasher.

"And just what do you suggest?" Christy felt angry that her mom was hurting and she didn't have a clue about what she could do to handle it.

"I think it's time we had a heart to heart with a certain officer of the law." Kate handed Christy the detergent and watched while Christy placed it in the dishwasher, secured the door and turned it on.

All three of them stood facing each other while they dried their hands and didn't say another word, yet all were in agreement about their next step.

Nancy came back into the kitchen and announced she was ready. "See you guys later! Love you!"

"Love you, Mom!"

Christy and Jackson watched as Nancy and Kate walked out to the car.

"Babe, promise me we'll never get that nuts with our relationship." Jackson put his arm around Christy's waist.

"Oh, we will. But we'll get over it because we love each other." Christy rested her head on Jackson's shoulder.

They watched the car pull away.

Then Christy said something that she knew would make Jackson change the expression on his face.

"Honey, let's go through the bridal magazine – again." And was rewarded with his look of dismay. "Just kidding."

CHAPTER 23

By the time Kate and Nancy reached downtown, Nancy was actually feeling better. She guessed the nap and food helped. It took them almost ten minutes to find a parking spot because of the holiday traffic. By the time they got out of the car they already knew exactly which stores they were going to hit and in what order.

The holiday decorations and lights made the historical downtown area look festive and the piped in music also helped raise Nancy's mood. Why did stores start decorating for Christmas in November, anyway?

They were heading for their first stop when the best smell in the whole world hit them. They turned and looked at each other and knew without speaking what was going to happen next.

"Gingerbread!" They both laughed and headed to the Gingerbread Hut for dessert. The bread was made fresh every two hours and was topped with your choice of either real whipped cream or a lemon hard sauce.

Nancy and Kate got both.

They found a corner table and were soon enjoying their treat.

By the time they'd finished and licked all the gooey sweetness off their fingers, Nancy felt better than she had for quite a while. She didn't particularly enjoy shopping, but she enjoyed Kate's company.

They threw away their trash and headed for the first stop of many. Nancy found just the right teaching gift for Tess as Kate browsed through the card section. After paying for Tess' beaded apple-shaped ornament, they exited the store and turned left.

Next stop, the high-end lingerie boutique where Kate bought Christy a cute pajama set with matching slippers. Nancy looked through the lingerie section and wondered if she'd ever feel the need to purchase something sexy again. Which brought her thoughts back to Doug. Nancy sighed but by the time Kate was ready to leave the store, she had once more reined in her emotions.

As they walked down the festive crowded street, Nancy was once again struck with how many couples were shopping. It seemed like everywhere she looked, a man and a woman were either arm in arm or having a conversation. Some were young, some were old. Nancy watched a couple that looked to be about her age and wondered why they could make it work, but she couldn't. What was wrong with her anyway?

She knew she wasn't ugly. Nancy thought she looked better now that she'd cut out sugar and white flour (well except for the gingerbread) and had dropped about eight pounds. She also knew that with make-up and jewelry, she looked pretty good for her age. Then why wasn't some guy falling head over heels for her?

As they entered their next stop, a handsome man about 10 years younger than Nancy held the door for them. They both thanked him, but Kate was the only one who noticed how his gaze lingered on Nancy after she passed by him. Kate shook her head. Her mom just didn't see the guys who checked her out. She'd tried to tell her mom about the men who had tried flirting with Nancy, but Nancy scoffed at Kate and told her she was reading things into innocent remarks. Boy! Could her mom be dense sometimes!

Nancy and Kate went in together for Jackson's gift, a lounge chair that had a built-in back and foot massage feature. Luckily it came in two boxes, assembly required, so they could take it with them.

Nancy also found a great saddlebag that would go perfect with Doug's motorcycle. Again her thoughts had turned to Doug. She mentally chided herself. This is ridiculous!

A grown woman, for gosh sakes, mooning over some guy. Well, maybe not just some guy, but a modern day hero in armor. Okay, okay. Kevlar to be precise.

"That would go good with Doug's bike." Kate spoke out loud what Nancy had only thought. "We could get it for him, you know." Nancy almost gave in.

"Honey, I'm not sure we'll ever see him again." Nancy had to choke the words out from around the huge lump that had formed at the base of her throat.

"Mom. You really need to call him. I could tell watching you two today that there is still something there between you. Neither of you looked happy. Please call him!" Kate was using her best powers of persuasion.

"I just can't, Kate. I was raised where the men called the women, not the other way around. I know that sounds old fashioned, but it's just the way I am."

"Yeah, mom. But you're forgetting the fact that old fashioned women also knew how to bake a casserole and take it to the guy they were interested in. At the very least they knew how to drop a hanky." With that final statement, Kate pretended to walk like she was wearing a corset and floor length gown, and dropped a woman's handkerchief behind her with a coy shifting of the eyes.

Nancy couldn't help but smile at her daughter's antics. She guessed that the acting gene HAD passed on to her offspring.

She laughed and watched Kate's eyes release some of their worry.

The remainder of their shopping went well and they had everything purchased and in the trunk of the car before 9:00 p.m.

Nancy wished that she'd actually bought the motorcycle saddlebags for Doug, even if they weren't going to continue their relationship. She knew how good it would look on the bike.

Kate hoped that her mom was so preoccupied that she hadn't noticed her buying the saddlebags and arranging for their delivery. Somehow, someway, Kate vowed to get her mom and Doug back together again. She hadn't ever seen her mom as happy as when she and Doug had been together.

CHAPTER 24

The next few days dragged past in exquisite torture. Nancy just couldn't stop thinking about Doug and wishing that he'd change his mind and call her.

She tried to make sense of what was happening. Several times she was sure that when the phone rang, it was Doug calling to apologize to her, but it was just one of her girls' friends. Nancy tried to imagine the amount of pressure and stress that Doug was under. Going through the trial must be horrendous. However, trying to empathize did nothing for her heart.

She still held out hope that he would call. In her more sane moments, she was certain that what they had between them was more than just a fling. She could almost feel him thinking about her.

In her less sane moments, her imagination came up with every awful thought that it could. Nancy was certain that Doug hadn't really cared for her at all. She'd even convinced herself that the bouquet had been a 'good-bye, thanks for the good time" gift.

Thanksgiving Day was the worst!

She'd wanted to invite Doug over for Thanksgiving dinner. Her kids had been nagging her about calling Doug. But she just couldn't bring herself to do it.

Nancy really didn't want to look like a pest, or worse, desperate. When she still hadn't heard from Doug by the Monday before Thanksgiving, she called her folks and asked if she could bring the girls and all the food up to their house and fix Thanksgiving meal for everyone.

Her family was more than happy to have Nancy and the girls. So, they packed everything into the car late Wednesday night and drove to Redlands. Her girls tried once again to get her to call Doug, but she refused.

Nancy thought she'd done a pretty good job of looking cheerful for Thanksgiving. If any of Nancy's family thought she looked sad, they didn't say anything. Kate and Christy had filled everyone in on Nancy's situation, so the topic of Doug had not been brought up at all.

It didn't make the day move by any faster, but at least Nancy was kept busy in the kitchen. When it came time for the family prayer circle, it took everything Nancy had to not start crying -- again. During the prayer, she made a point to mentally sing something so that she wouldn't hear the word "thankful" and start crying. However, when the mental song turned into a slow love ballad by *Alabama*, Nancy felt her eyes fill. Thank goodness the prayer was over and she could run to the bathroom before serving the dinner. Sometimes the excuse of "hot flash" was useful.

Nancy didn't see her family exchange looks with each other at the table. And after dinner when her mom and dad had a talk with her girls, she missed that one too.

Everyone left the house with foil packages and bags of food. Invariably, there was always too much food left over. Usually Nancy and the girls would take the food down to the San Bernardino courthouse area where the homeless seemed to congregate, and they'd distribute the food packages.

However, this year, Nancy just didn't have it in her. Instead she pleaded a headache and went to bed early. Usually she felt comfortable at her folks' house and slept soundly. However, this time she tossed and turned until the clock said 3:30 am, at which time she gave up and padded out to the darkened living room and quietly put on a movie to watch.

Unfortunately, her choice was "An Affair to Remember" with Cary Grant and Debra Kerr. Oh well. At least she had a reasonable excuse for tears if someone happened to stumble upon her.

The next day, she and girls drove with her mom and dad up to Oak Glen and enjoyed the local petting zoo and once again stuffed themselves with even more pie than the evening before. One cannot go to Oak Glen without having apple pie.

That evening they enjoyed a family game of Scrabble until once again Nancy begged off and went to bed early. She didn't think her family knew she saw the looks they gave her when she supposedly wasn't watching.

Luckily, they knew her well enough to not be sympathetic. That would have been her complete undoing, and she really needed to pull it together.

On Sunday, she and the girls drove home. She knew it would have been too good to be true if there was a note or something left at her house. Maybe a black and white unit?

But there wasn't anything.

Luckily there was a ton of laundry to do before school started again the next day, and Nancy also decided to clean out the pantry area – again.

Kate left the house after getting a phone call and Jackson had shown up and taken Christy to the movies.

Nancy had the house to herself. The quiet, dead house.

To quote one of her newer students "life sucks."

CHAPTER 25

Andy's case went to trial. With Attorney Harris' legal expertise and Andy's show of changed behavior, Andy was sentenced to the time he'd already spent in jail, and was told he had a rather hefty fine and had been assigned several hours of community service working at the homeless shelter for the two weeks prior to Christmas and Christmas Day itself.

Doug volunteered to work a double shift on Thanksgiving Day. He hoped that he would be too busy to think about Nancy. Wishful thinking. It seemed like she was ALL he thought about.

Bill had told him he was being a horse's ass, and that he should go see Nancy. Doug had tried to explain why he couldn't, but Bill and Patty weren't buying any of it. Doug couldn't even truly explain it to himself.

However, he knew that if Nancy was still interested in him, she would have called.

Bill and Patty all but disowned him, which made it even harder.

Thanksgiving afternoon was busy. Mostly with older people who had no family to help celebrate the holiday. Around 5:00 pm there was a lull. Doug spent the down time working up the courage to stop by Nancy's and apologize. He drove past her street several times. Finally he turned onto the street and drove slowly towards her house.

Reluctantly, he pulled the black and white unit into her driveway and took a deep breath while he turned off the engine.

Doug got out of the car and walked towards the door rehearsing what he was going to say.

He knocked.

And waited.

No answer.

He knocked again.

And waited.

He stepped into the bushes at the front of the house and was looking into the kitchen window, when the neighbor lady called out.

"They're not home. They took off last night."

"Did they say where they were going?" Doug tried not to look embarrassed while he stepped out of the bushes and onto the walkway.

The neighbor was dressed in brown polyester slacks, an orange blouse and an apron which said "Turkey Day!" emblazoned with a cartoon of a turkey running from a man with a hatchet.

"Nope. But I think I heard one of the girls say something about being away for a few days."

Doug's spirits dropped even lower than before.

"Thank you for your help. Have a nice Thanksgiving, Ma'am." Doug walked back to his unit and slid in behind the wheel. He sat there looking at Nancy's house until he realized that the neighbor lady with the awful apron was still watching him.

He started the engine, put the car into reverse and touched the brim of his cap at the lady as he drove past her down the street.

Doug wished he'd called Nancy. He wished it wasn't Thanksgiving and he wished the day would move faster.

Where'd they go?

Maybe she went to her parents?

Was it just her and her kids?

The day dragged on.

As did the next few days. For some reason Doug just couldn't bring himself to get up the courage to call Nancy again or stop by.

Coward! He chastised himself. What would it take to get him to call? Hell, he was a cop. He was supposed to be brave and courageous. Yeah. Right now he'd rather face a 6'4" 275 pound guy on crack than look into Nancy's eyes and see absolutely nothing.

He wasn't even looking forward to dinner at Bill and Patty's house that evening. He knew they would put him through the ringer six ways to Sunday. Hell, maybe he deserved it. Call it penance.

When he arrived at their front door at five minutes to 8:00 that evening, Doug made sure he had gifts in hand; flowers for Patty and a bottle of Rancho Mirage Aged Port for Bill.

"Oh, Doug! They're beautiful!" Patty gave him a hug and then took the flowers into the kitchen, looking for a vase.

Doug held out the bottle of port to Bill. Bill just stood there with his arms crossed over his chest.

"Ah. Common, Bill. It's a gift. Accept it graciously." Doug was trying to sound lighthearted, but his comment came out more like a dig.

"Have you come to your senses yet?" Bill leaned forward slightly and pinned Doug with his stare.

Doug felt as though he was standing in front of the sergeant and being dressed down for some infraction. He didn't like it one bit.

"Come on, Bill. Cut me some slack."

"What sort of friend would I be if I did that? Doug, you know that I rarely step in and tell you what to do."

At Doug's raised eyebrow, Bill shifted slightly and changed his tactics.

"Doug, you know that Patty and I love you like family, right?"

Doug nodded in affirmation and tried to curb his exasperation.

"Patty and I just think that if you let this woman go, you'll regret it for the rest of your life. I don't want to see that happen."

"I know, Bill. I know."

Doug looked so forlorn, that Bill took pity on him, and taking the bottle of wine, led Doug into the family room for dinner. There they joined Patty and the kids, twin sixteen year old boys Eric and Kenny. Eric was quarterback of Orange High's winning football team. His brother Kenny was the editor of the high school newspaper, *The Panther*. Both boys were above-average students, as well as being two of the most popular men on campus. Thank goodness they were also ethical. They'd inherited their dads' moral compass and their mom's compassion.

Now Doug found himself under the scrutiny of this family, which had no desire to mind its own business.

When the conversation finally lulled at one point, Doug was surprised to hear Kenny say, "Uncle Doug. I don't understand what's stopping you from calling Nancy. If she's as wonderful as it sounds like she is, and you feel as strongly as you seem to, you need to go for it. The worst that will happen is that she'll turn you down."

Doug was hard pressed to even explain it to himself, much less to these people who cared so much about him.

Eric joined in. "Yeah, Uncle Doug. It's really better to at least try than not to try and forever regret that you didn't.

Good grief! When high school boys understood better what he should do than he did himself, he knew he was in trouble.

What had ever happened to the love-em-and-leave-em guy he used to be? When had it all gotten so complicated?

His gut twisted when he answered his own question. It had all gotten complicated when he'd fallen in love. He truly loved Nancy. He felt more for her than he'd ever felt for anyone else in his life. It might be a cliché, but she completed him. She made him feel that he could do anything he wanted. He felt that she made him a better man.

While Doug mulled over these thoughts, Bill, Patty and the boys went about dinner as though Doug was an active participant.

When Doug finally left for the evening, Patty handed him a bag of leftovers to take home.

She kissed him on the cheek and whispered, "Doug, don't make a mistake with Nancy. At least have dinner with her."

Doug gave her a kiss back and thanked her for the great dinner. He shook Bill's hand and gave a playful punch on the arms of both the boys, trying to appear himself.

Except, the sad fact was that "himself" was now an empty shell. He really didn't know what he was going to do.

....

"If someone doesn't do something about this, I'm going to go crazy!" Jackson was pacing around the kitchen.

Kate and Christy were putting away groceries.

"Okay. Tell us what to do and we'll do it!" Kate replied with a snap in her voice.

"Hey! Don't get angry at Jackson! It's not his fault!" Christy was instantly defensive.

Reluctantly Kate walked over to Jackson and gave him a hug. "I'm sorry, Bro. This is just a really bad situation and it's got me on edge."

Jackson patted her on the back. "It's okay. I understand." Christy smiled at Jackson.

"So what DO we do?" Christy put the ice cream into the freezer next to the frozen veggies.

"I already talked with Mom and she'd adamant about not calling the police station again. I told her that she'd only called once and just maybe Doug hadn't gotten the call. But she insisted that he wasn't interested in her anymore and at least she'd have her pride." Kate explained.

"Yeah, but pride won't keep you warm on a cold night." Jackson just shook his head.

Just then Kate's cell phone rang. She pulled it out of her front pocket and looked at who was calling. You'd think that she'd just been told she'd won the lottery! She jumped once, grinned from ear to ear and leaving the room said "Catch you guys later!" Then softly, "Hello?"

Jackson looked at Christy with eyebrows raised in question.

Christy looked back at him with a negative shake of her head indicating that she had no idea who was on the phone. "I don't think it was Robert, though. She dumped him a couple of days ago."

"Really? What stupid move did this one make?" Jackson enjoyed watching Kate go through boyfriends. It always made him feel even better about his relationship with Christy.

"I believe he was critical of his parents." Christy grinned back at Jackson. "Or, it could have been that he sided with the oppressors of any third world country, or he stated that he didn't think there was anything wrong with hunting small animals for sport. Take your pick."

"Babe, tell me again that we're never going to split-up." Jackson held Christy lightly in his arms.

"Babe, we're never going to split-up." Christy smiled sweetly.

"Unless you do something really stupid." Christy teased him.

Jackson tightened his arms. "Don't EVER kid about that. I mean it."

Christy could see just how much this had affected Jackson.

"Don't worry, babe. Never again. You are my guy forever."

"Damn right." Jackson hugged her hard.

PAT ADEFF

CHAPTER 26

"Doug! Someone is here to speak with you."

The desk officer called down the hall to where Doug had been filling out the endless pile of paperwork from that weekend. It seemed that the weekend just before Christmas was always the busiest.

Doug had thought that the paperwork would have gotten less with the department having moved into the computer age. However, it seemed like there were now more forms than ever! Doug loved police work. He just wasn't a big fan of the paper chase. Which was the reason he was still a cop with a beat. Several years back when he'd been promoted to a desk job, he'd suffered through it for one year, finally took the pay cut and went back to the streets.

Doug finished the sentence he'd been writing, stood up and went to the front desk area.

And stopped.

Standing there were Kate, Christy and Jackson. All three had their arms folded across their chests and were not smiling.

"Hi, there!" Doug stood on the other side of the half-wall and waited for one of them to speak.

"What exactly were your intentions regarding Mom?" Christy was the first to speak up and it was not in a friendly tone of voice.

"Yeah. Why haven't you called her?" Kate's tone was not any better.

"Did you just get what you wanted and then dumped her?" Jackson spoke up, too.

By this time, there was a small group of smiling officers paying attention to the conversation, and Doug was not about to answer any of these questions with an audience.

"Would you guys like to go get a cup of coffee with me and we'll talk?" Doug had the desk officer buzz him through to the lobby area and he closed the door behind him, so it was just the kids and him.

Kate and Christy looked at each other. Christy looked at Jackson, and all three looked at Doug.

"Okay. You're buying." Kate answered.

"Of course. Let's go to the cafe next door." Doug led them out of the police station and they walked the half-block to the small cafe in silence.

They found an empty booth and ordered coffee. Christy and Jackson sat on one side of the booth, and Kate begrudgingly sat on the other side next to Doug. She seemed to be perched on just three inches at the end of the booth.

Doug indicated she could scoot closer, but Kate just shook her head "no" as though he had cooties or something.

Christy was the first one to speak up.

"You made Mom cry."

With that declaration, she'd put the ball into Doug's court. All three of the kids sat there looking at him like he was some kind of bug that needed to be stepped on.

"I don't think you understand what you're talking about," Doug replied.

"That's a load of bull." Jackson was actually angry.

"We know exactly what we're talking about." Kate was trying to stay level-headed, but Doug could hear the hurt and anger under her calm demeanor. "First Dad hurts her, then you do. Why don't you want to be with her anymore?"

Doug was stunned into silence for a moment. Not want to be with her?! He'd give anything if she'd ask him back.

"See? You don't care!" Christy was vehement.

"She doesn't want me." Doug wasn't sure if he gave voice to his thought or if Kate could read his mind.

"She thinks you don't want HER!" Kate had just about had enough of dense men. "Why did you stop seeing her?" Doug thought to himself that if she wanted, Kate could have a successful career as a police investigator. He'd seen the same look that was in her eyes in some of the force's best cops.

"This is going to sound lame." Doug figured things couldn't get any worse, so he decided to bare his soul.

"Try us." Christy's tone left Doug in no doubt that whatever came out of his mouth next needed to be really, REALLY good.

"I got so involved in Andy's legal case and trying to make amends to him and Sue that by the time I came up for air, it was really awkward to call Nancy. Since she hadn't tried to reach me, I figured she was no longer interested."

"What do you mean? She called and left a message for you several weeks ago!" Jackson wasn't buying it yet.

Doug was puzzled. "When did she call? I never got any message. I swear it!"

Kate took pity on him. "I believe you." She looked at Christy and Jackson. "I tried to get her to call again, but she said that he'd call her if he wanted to."

"You mean she's been waiting for me to call her?"

"Look. We understand that this is a modern society and women call men all the time, but Mom is basically an old-fashioned girl at heart. You need to pursue her, not the other way around." Now Jackson was giving Doug dating tips.

"That's exactly what Patty said." Doug thought out loud to himself.

"Who's Patty?" Christy was once again on the offense.

"My best friend's wife. The two of them have practically written me off. Patty told me that I should just call Nancy, but I didn't believe her." Doug looked back at the comedy of errors that had been building between Nancy and himself. He shook his head slowly back and forth.

They sat there waiting for his next move.

Doug finally pulled himself from his thoughts and looked expectantly at the kids. "Is it too late?"

They looked back at him as slow smiles started to cover their faces.

Kate added, "And if you can follow directions, there's even a very nice Christmas gift for you."

****

Nancy had just pulled the turkey from the oven for Christmas Eve dinner. Both her girls would be there any minute, along with Jackson. She knew that she should be grateful for her wonderful family and she was. However, she'd lost her sense of enthusiasm and was sort of moving along day to day. She missed Doug horribly, but understood that it was better for him to be back with Sue and his son, Andy. That's what a family was supposed to be. Together.

There was a knock at the front door.

"Just a minute!" Nancy shouted to whoever was at the door. She wiped her hands dry with the kitchen towel and opened the door.

Then she just stared.

Broad navy-blue shoulders filled her field of vision.

Mirrored sunglasses glinted in the sunlight.

The badge flashed as he reached up to pull off the sunglasses.

Familiar dark blue, almost black eyes met hers before cutting to Nancy's right hand where the kitchen towel had once again slipped from her fingers and fallen to the ground.

Nancy pulled herself out of the spell she'd fallen under and reached down for the towel at the same time Doug reached for it. They ended up bumping shoulders. Nancy started to fall sideways but was stopped when she felt strong his strong warm hands grab her shoulders and help her stand upright.

They stood there like that, staring into each other's eyes. The hurt and the longing were almost unbearable.

Doug pulled his hands from Nancy's shoulders.

"May I come in? Please?"

Nancy stared at Doug. Her heart was beating a hundred miles a minute. Could he hear it?

"Of course. Come on in." She stood back while he filled the entry hall and once again took all the oxygen.

Nancy moved into the kitchen and tried to breathe. "Would you like some coffee?"

"Coffee sounds great." Doug kept watching her, waiting for a sign of some sort.

Nancy poured two cups from the freshly brewed pot and placed one of them at the end of the kitchen table and one of them at the seat to the right.

Doug put his cap on the other end of the table and sat down. Nancy sat down next to him. They both sipped from their cups, looking over the rims at each other, drinking in each other's face.

Doug cleared his throat and launched into the speech he'd rehearsed over and over as though his life depended on it. In fact, it did. "Nancy, you deserved better than this from me."

She really didn't want to hear what she was afraid he was going to say and interrupted him. "It's okay, Doug. I understand. Families should be together." It sounded right. Too bad the words made her heart hurt enough to crack in two.

"I'm sorry I didn't call sooner. Once the trial was over, it was so awkward for me and I wasn't sure you'd want to hear from me again." Doug wished with all his heart that he could find the magic words that would bring Nancy back into his life.

There was a pause, as they both sipped on the coffee that neither of them was tasting.

"So, are you and Sue going to get married now?" Nancy grimaced. She'd sworn to herself that she wasn't going to ask that question.

"What?" Doug could see where Nancy's thoughts had erroneously gone to. "Of course not. Sue and I are just friends. Don't misunderstand me. It's good to have her friendship back. But it's not like that. We've come to an understanding as Andy's parents and she has forgiven me for not doing my job as a dad." Doug waited several seconds for a reply from Nancy.

When none came, he quietly asked "Can *you* ever forgive me?"

Nancy thought her throat would never open up enough for her to say the words. "I thought you'd gone back to Sue." Then the tears started. She hated when she cried like that.

The tears were Doug's undoing. "Aw, Nancy. Don't cry. Please don't cry." He reached for her but Nancy pushed him away.

She rushed to her feet as weeks of torment bubbled to the surface and burst out of her. "You jerk!" Nancy swiped at her tears and couldn't have stopped what she was spouting, even if you'd offered her a million bucks. "Do you have any idea how awful it's been for me? I finally open up to someone – YOU – and I get dumped! It's humiliating and degrading. I've never felt this badly about myself EVER! I was better off before you entered my life. It HURTS loving you!"

Doug just sat there dumbfounded. Out of all that verbiage, he was pinning his hope on that last sentence. She loved him! A slow grin spread across his face.

Nancy couldn't believe what she was seeing. Doug thought this was funny! Oh, it made her FURIOUS! "Get out! Leave here now!" She strode to the door and had it already open by the time Doug reached her.

He slowly put his hand on the door and shut it. Then he moved closer to Nancy, inches from her. She could feel the heat radiating from him. He made her knees weak, but she was NOT going to give into her attraction to him. Not now. She needed to hang onto the last shred of self-preservation she had.

Doug's voice was low and gravely. "Do you have any idea what I'VE been through? Do you?" He put his hand under her chin and raised her face, so she'd look at him. "You've made me into a man I don't recognize. I'm no longer relaxed and carefree. I spend inordinate amounts of my day thinking about you. Missing you. Wanting you. I drive past your house and school dozens of times a week, wondering what you're doing. I've called myself all kinds of a fool. But guess what?"

When Nancy didn't say anything, he nudged her chin up a tiny bit more, so she'd have to look straight into his eyes.

He repeated his question. "Guess what?"

Nancy was finally able to say something past the lump in her throat. "What?" As the word whispered out of her mouth it also unleashed more tears. God, she hated it when she cried!

"I realized I would rather be a fool with you, than be my old self without you. Nancy, I love you. I know you love me. I want us to make this work."

When she just stood there silently staring at him, he took a deep breath and gave it everything he had in him.

"I need you in my life. When I'm with you, I feel like I can conquer the world. Without you, I'm lost. I ..."

Nancy felt her soul come back to life. Doug wanted her! She put her fingertips on his lips.

"Just kiss me," she whispered.

Doug smiled and slowly placed kisses across her brow, across her face and finally on her lips. He whispered against her mouth, "Don't cry. I'm so sorry. Please forgive me. I can't live without you. I need you."

Then he claimed her mouth fully. His lips seeking forgiveness and redemption.

Nancy felt like a bright light had started to shine in her heart and was threatening to burst out of her chest. He needed her as much as she needed him!

"Oh, Doug! I thought you didn't want me anymore. I thought you were through with me. My life felt over." She said, speaking against his mouth between kisses.

Doug pulled back and gently cupped Nancy's precious face between his hands.

"Darling, I'll love you and need you until the day I die. Will you put up with me even when I'm old and grumpy? Can you possibly love me even a fraction of how much I love you?"

Nancy's eyes filled with happy tears this time as she smiled. "I'll love you forever, even when you're old and grumpy. I'll love you until I die."

Doug looked deep into Nancy's eyes and recognized what he'd been looking for his whole life. As his mouth slowly lowered to hers again, he vowed to protect and serve her for the rest of his life.

Sometime during the kiss, Doug became aware of the kitchen filling with people. He and Nancy broke apart and smiled sheepishly at Kate, Christy and Jackson standing here, once again grinning like the village idiots.

"So, are you guys going to behave like grown-ups now, or what?" Christy was unable to make her statement sound anything other than pleased.

While Nancy untangled herself from Doug's embrace with as much dignity as she could muster, she started to lodge a protest with Christy's mouthy comment, but stopped when she realized Christy was totally right! It was a little mortifying to realize that she HAD been acting like a moonstruck teenager, instead of a mature mother of two.

"Alright, everyone. Help me get dinner on the table. Then we'll talk."

Cheerful chatter filled the kitchen while everyone followed Nancy's orders, and soon the table was laden with turkey, mashed potatoes, gravy, buttered baby peas, sweet potato casserole, warm Italian bread rolls with butter and honey, with a pumpkin pie resting on the counter for dessert.

They all stood around the table holding hands for grace and one for one looked towards Doug.

"Me?" They all nodded 'yes.'

Doug didn't think he would be able to handle any more emotion. He remembered a prayer his father used to say at special occasions just like this.

He bowed his head and the others followed his lead. While Nancy, Kate, Christy and Jackson held hands around the table, Doug repeated the prayer. When they were done he looked up to find Nancy's eyes shining at him. He felt as though he'd just been accepted into this wonderful family completely.

As they all cheerfully sat down ready to dig in, the kids started firing questions at Nancy and Doug. At first they tried to answer but ended up just sitting there smiling at each other while the questions flew around the table.

Nancy found that she and Doug didn't have to answer anything, since the kids were answering their own questions.

So they just enjoyed the wonderful dinner.

EPILOGUE

"Mom, you look beautiful." Kate and Christy were standing behind Nancy as she looked at herself in the full-length mirror in Bill and Patty's guest room.

Nancy felt beautiful. Her soft green and ecru tea length dress flattered her curves. The sweetheart neckline was the perfect frame for the heart-shaped locket that was Doug's wedding gift to her. The girls, Jackson and Doug had found the time to get their picture taken together and the locket now held that same picture; close to her heart. Small gold hoop earrings with tiny pearls were the only other jewelry Nancy wore.

Kate and Christy both looked wonderful in similar cut dresses but different darker hues of green to match their own skin tones.

Their small bouquets sat on the dresser next to Nancy's bouquet of white roses and orange blossoms.

"Does Pops have his boutonniere?" Nancy asked again.

"Yes, Mom, he does. Still." Christy shared a smile with Kate.

Just then there was a knock at the bedroom door, and Patty came in. "Well, the guests are all seated and I think that man of yours is chomping at the bit to get started."

Patty and Bill had been wonderful about letting Doug and Nancy use their garden for the wedding. Patty had used the opportunity to have her whole backyard redone; including having a rock fountain installed by Johnny's Landscaping, which looked like a waterfall, as well as building a gazebo that was big enough to hold a ten piece orchestra.

The fact that she'd also used her and Bill's wedding vows renewal ceremony as a second excuse helped.

She and Bill had repeated their vows with just the minister, their sons, Doug and Nancy and her girls and Jackson. It had been perfect beyond words. That evening, Bill had taken her to a small bed and breakfast in Laguna Niguel and they'd stayed the weekend. Patty smiled just thinking about it.

Now, she handed the girls their bouquets and then smiling, presented Nancy's to her. Nancy felt such joy in the new friendship she's found with Patty. It was good to know she had a cop's wife as her friend. It would make Nancy's transition into that role much easier; although Nancy felt she'd done pretty good so far.

They all went downstairs and made their way to the back door which opened onto the backyard. The very crowded back yard.

Nancy's breath caught in her throat. Who were all these people? She'd only invited her and Doug's families and some of their co-workers from the school and police department. However, the yard was wall to wall people. So much for a small intimate wedding.

Patty laughed. "It sure filled up fast, didn't it! It's a good thing I decided to have the party rental place leave extra chairs, huh?"

Something about the way Patty said this made Nancy think she'd known all along how many people were coming to this shindig. Nancy turned to Patty to ask her about it, but just then the music started.

Nancy's niece was playing guitar and singing the song that Nancy and Doug had danced to on their first date.

Patty kissed Nancy on the cheek and then went down the three steps and Bill met her there, walking her down the aisle to their seats. The aisle was formed by white folding chairs on either side, leading to the gazebo. Patty was very happy with the results. Of course, she'd had to ride the construction and garden workers like a drill sergeant in order to get everything done in time. But, hey, that was the sort of thing she lived for.

Nancy watched as first Christy and then Kate walked slowly down the aisle towards the gazebo. Her heart overflowed with love as she watched these two beautiful young women. She was so lucky to have her family.

As Nancy moved to the top of the steps, her dad stepped forward and held out his elbow for Nancy to take. Since the heart surgery he'd done so much better. He and Nancy's mom, who was sitting in the front row beaming at her granddaughters, had even taken several trips in their new RV, traveling across America.

They'd made it home three weeks ago in time for the wedding, but had plans to take off again next weekend, heading for an RV park in northern California where Nancy's mom would be able to feed the new baby lambs with a bottle. After that, her dad said they were thinking of traveling to New Zealand and renting an RV down there. She was so happy for her folks.

Nancy slipped her hand through her dad's elbow and looked up to the end of the aisle where the wedding party was standing.

The police department chaplain was officiating and looked outstanding in his dress uniform. On the far right, Jackson was standing opposite Christy as a groomsman. Next to him, Andy was Doug's best man and looked like a best man. He'd gone through rehab with flying colors and was now enrolled at the local college for police science classes. Across the aisle from Andy was Kate, looking radiant and giving a small wave to her new boyfriend, Dr. Coburn, who was sitting behind Nancy's mom. Derek waved back at Kate.

Nancy looked at Doug and started to smile at him when suddenly everyone stood up and she lost sight of him behind the sea of shoulders and heads.

Nancy felt like the aisle was a mile long! Finally as she and her dad got to the end of it, she was able to see Doug again.

He was waiting for her at the base of the steps leading up into the gazebo. Nancy turned to her dad and gave him a kiss on the cheek. Then she turned and put her hand into Doug's outstretched one and he pulled her next to him.

Doug looked so handsome in his three piece suit. He'd debated on whether to wear his dress uniform, because he knew what the uniform did for Nancy. But they decided on the suit instead.

It still made Doug's breath catch when he remembered the time that Nancy had made him stand there while she undressed him, vest and all. Then, she'd undressed herself – very slowly – until he thought he'd go mad. They'd tumbled to his bed, lost in each other's arms until the small hours of the morning. Now, he looked down at her and thought he was the luckiest man on the earth.

As Nancy and Doug turned and looked fully into each other's face, their bond of love strengthened even more. Their hands clasped tightly.

When Doug repeated the words after the Chaplain, his eyes misted and he had to clear his throat, he was so overcome with emotion.

Nancy was just as emotional as Doug and found her hands trembling as she put a matching plain gold band on Doug's left hand.

Soon the ceremony was done and the beaming Chaplain informed Doug that he could kiss the bride.

Nancy should have known that this was not going to be any civilized peck on the cheek.

Nope. To the accompanying applause from their guests, Doug

kissed Nancy thoroughly, tenderly, earnestly. Finally, Doug drew his face back from hers and looked into her eyes.

"I love you, Nancy Saunders. I will love you for the rest of my life."

"I love you, Doug. Husband." The word felt and sounded perfect.

Kate gave Nancy her bouquet and hand in hand Nancy and Doug moved down the aisle, receiving handshakes and good wishes from their friends.

The reception started promptly at Patty's urging, and the music was loud and the speeches even louder.

Nancy was very happy to see Kate and Dr. Coburn dancing and talking throughout the afternoon. She laughed when she saw Derek do some card tricks for the kids who'd come with their folks.

Christy and Jackson danced almost every dance and then disappeared, only to reappear right about the time Nancy threw the bouquet. Surprisingly, and delightfully, Sue caught the bouquet!

When the photographer had Nancy and Sue pose together, Nancy was happy to have Sue's sincere congratulations. She didn't think they'd ever be close friends, but she was glad to be on good terms with Doug's son's mother. It would make everything easier for them all.

When it came time for the Bride and Groom to leave the party, they were showered with bird seed and climbed into Doug's truck which seemed to have every single can from the supermarket attached to its back bumper.

Doug stopped on the next block and they spent a couple of minutes removing the noise-makers.

****

Later that night, Nancy lay curled against Doug with her left hand splayed across his bare chest. Her fingers were writing 'I love you' and drawing hearts on his skin.

They'd left the reception while it was still in full swing and driven up the mountain to a bed and breakfast at Lake Arrowhead. Doug had reserved the honeymoon suite, which consisted of a large bedroom which housed a king size bed, a balcony that overlooked the lake, and a private bathroom with a king size jacuzzi bathtub.

Doug and Nancy had tried out the bathtub in lieu of dinner. But now, two hours later, after having made it from the bathtub to the bed, Nancy could hear both her and Doug's stomachs growl.

"Hungry?" Doug looked down at the top of Nancy's head while she continued to write on his chest.

"Starving!" Nancy looked up into Doug's face and lifted her lips for another soul-shaking kiss. The kiss deepened and his hand moved down her arm and covered her breast.

She arched and pushed into his hand. The electricity moved through her body. Doug enveloped her and pulled her underneath him while he continued to kiss her thoroughly, then trailed kisses down her throat. His right hand moved down her left side, feeling the smooth silk of her skin.

The roughness of the skin of his hand was a delightful complement to her softness and warmth.

Nancy's breath caught and it was all she could do to hold on to his broad warm shoulders while he continued making love to her. He knew her body so well.

Doug again lost himself in Nancy. It took him quite a while until his heartbeat died down and the sweat on his back started to cool him off.

He shifted to his side and pulled Nancy up against him until her head rested on his shoulder and her arm was once again across his chest.

After who knew how long, Doug fondly slapped Nancy's hip, sat up on the side of the bed, and grabbed her hand, pulling her from the bed. "Come on, woman. Let's get some food. We'll need our energy."

Laughing, Nancy and Doug showered quickly and dressed in jeans and pull-over sweatshirts that said "Bride" on hers and "Groom" on his.

The sweatshirts were one of the corny gifts they'd received at Nancy's bridal shower. However, Nancy didn't think she'd EVER wear the tee-shirt that was her half of the set that Doug had been given at his bachelor party. Well, maybe around the house, if no company was expected, and it was completely dark.

It was still relatively early, 8:00 pm, and they found the restaurant next door was still serving dinner. They had salads and huge steaks that covered their plates. They were both famished and laughed at how much food they put away.

As they finished up a piece of apple pie they'd split, the band started up in the lounge of the restaurant.

Doug smiled at Nancy, stood up and pulled out his wallet. He left several bills on the table to cover dinner and a generous tip, and held Nancy's chair while she stood up.

Waving at their waitress, they went into the lounge and moved directly onto the dance floor. Moving slowly into Doug's arms, Nancy sighed with joy.

They danced for several dances and were for the most part the only dancers on the floor. After another slow dance Doug could hardly contain his emotion. He loved this woman so much.

He leaned back to look into her face. Her sweet face. He lowered his lips to hers and gently tasted her. She tasted of apple pie and happily ever after.

Nancy broke the kiss and smiled up into Doug's face. Her husband's wonderful face.

"So, Officer. Did you happen to bring the vest with you?"

Doug's breath caught.

The band members and several of the lounge patrons smiled and laughed as Doug scooped Nancy up into his arms and headed for the door, grinning.

As they left the restaurant, several people heard him say, "Honey, I live to serve."

THE END

ABOUT THE AUTHOR

Pat Adeff has diligently indulged her love of writing ever since picking up a pencil in Mrs. Shaner's 1st grade class at McKinley Elementary School in Redlands, CA. The author of 13 plays, of which 8 have been produced in community theatres across Southern California, Pat has earned several awards for her writing. She was the co-founder of an award-winning arts academy, as well as founding a youth theatre workshop that occurs every summer at the historic Redlands Footlighters Theatre. Her family has learned to live with her disappearing into her writing, and usually coming up for air several days (if not weeks) later. Pat has several more books in the works, a made-for-TV movie, as well as another play. She is an incurable romantic and definitely believes in happily-ever-afters, at any stage of life.

Being a writer, when confronted with her own divorce, she of course wrote! Although "To Protect and Serve" is definitely fiction, the seed of the story grew from her own personal turmoil and overcoming the ups and downs of life being a single parent. Having been an avid romance reader from the start, Pat wanted to give women everywhere a story that was wonderfully romantic, yet was real, down-to-earth, and heartwarming. According to her first reviews, she succeeded! Well, once this first romance was completed, all of a sudden romance stories came to her in droves! In fact, the stories wouldn't stop, and she finally had to list them all on a huge white board in her writing area, just so she could concentrate on one at a time. She's almost done with her next book which is about a writer (of course) and the geeky, but cute guy who fixes her computer when it crashes on her. It's amazing just how often that computer crashes! The third one, which is more than half-way written, is about a divorced legal secretary who finds herself falling for an established country-western singer. Although opposites in many ways, they definitely agree in some important areas, and work through the difficulties that naturally attend such a non-conforming mutual attraction. In romance parlance, they're hot for each other!

WHAT OTHERS ARE SAYING ABOUT
"To Protect and Serve."

REVIEW FROM TEXAS: *WOW! I just finished "To Protect and Serve" by Pat Adeff and what a ride! Lights flashing and sirens wailing! This was such a great read. I read it cover to cover in one sitting. I laughed, I cried and I couldn't put it down. Such a great story of a woman who fought for 20 years for a loveless marriage only to finally give up and find the man of her dreams. Good read. I highly recommend it!*

REVIEW FROM NEW JERSEY: *This book leaves out the romantic clichés and focuses on the experiences that are relatable to everyone. It's an easy to read, hard to put down love story with depth, humor, sweetness and spice! Would certainly recommend this to anyone who enjoys a good leisurely read!*

REVIEW FROM FLORIDA: *This is a great "Hey, it could really happen" type romance! Very down-to-earth and quite enjoyable, with a reality factor that seems to be missing from the average romance.*

REVIEW FROM ALASKA: *I would recommend this book to anyone who loves to read stories that leave them feeling good about life and that are artfully crafted.*

Pat's local "fan clubs" are based in Redlands, Yucaipa, Rialto and Grand Terrace, California, and include the FEMS (Female Entrepreneur Mavens) Dinner Network Group, led by Ms. Marsha Landeros, ARBONNE Independent Consultant, and Founded by Ms. Jenny Danforth, SOLAVEI Representative.

Made in the USA
Charleston, SC
27 March 2016